DIVINE
INTERVENTION

THE BATTLE BETWEEN GOOD AND EVIL

LYNWOOD MOORE

ISBN
978-1-962868-03-7 (Paperback)
978-1-962868-04-4 (eBook)
978-1-962868-02-0 (Hardcover)

The Forming of a Secret Government Background

During the years following World War II, the government of the United States was confronted with a change beyond its imagination. The future of humanity was about to be jarred like never before in our history.

A stunned President Truman and his military commanders suddenly found themselves virtually impotent. This feeling came after just winning the most devastating and costly war in history. The U.S. had developed and was the only nation on Earth in possession of the atomic bomb. Also, the atomic bomb had the potential to destroy any enemy and even including the Earth itself. At home we had the best economy, the most advanced technology, the highest standard of living, and we exerted the most influential, and the most powerful military forces in history. We can only imagine the confusion and concern, when the informed elite of the U.S. Government discovered that an alien spacecraft piloted by insect-like beings from a totally incomprehensible culture, had crashed in the desert of New Mexico.

Between January 1947 1952, there were at least sixteen crashed alien crafts, sixty-five alien bodies, and one live alien were recovered. Of those events, thirteen crashes occurred within the borders of the United States, not including one that disintegrated in the air. Sightings of UFOs were so numerous that serious investigations and debunking of each report became impossible, utilizing the intelligence assets. On February 13,1948, an alien craft was found on a mesa near Aztec, Arizona. Another craft was located on March25, 1948 in White Sands Proving Grounds It was 100 feet in diameter and a total of seventeen alien bodies were recovered from those two crafts. More disturbing was the many human body parts stored in both vehicles.

A demon had reared its head and paranoia had quickly taken hold of all those in the know. The secret had quickly become a Top-Secret Lid and was now screwed down tightly. In the coming years, these events now became the most closely guarded secrets in the history of the entire world.

During those early years, the United States Air Force and the Central Intelligence Agency exercised complete control over the Alien Secret. The CIA was formed by Presidential Executive Order first as the Central Intelligence Group with the express purpose of dealing with the alien presence. Later the National Security Act was passed, it was established as the Central Intelligence Agency. On December 9, 1949, President Harry Truman approved specific secretive measures that would control a buffer between the president and information being leaked to the sitting president. Secretary of Defense James Forrestal objected to the secrecy, Forrestal was a religious man and quite idealistic. He believed that the public should be kept well informed. The Defense Secretary would be the first abductee when he began talking to Congress about the alien problem. Truman asked him to resign. Forrestal expressed his fears that he was being overly watched. Others called it. Paranoia. He was soon said to have suffered a mental breakdown. He was ordered into the mental ward of Bethesda Naval Hospital. Without the authority the order was carried out. Forestall was then isolated and highly discredited. His friends were denied visits to him. Finally on May 21, 1949, Secretary of Defense Forrestal's brother in Florida decided that he was going to remove his brother from Bethesda Hospital. On May 22nd, 1949, when his brother from Florida arrived it was too late because early morning on May 22nd, 1949, CIA agents had reportedly tied a sheet around James Forrestal's neck and fastened the other end around a fixture in his room. Then his body was thrown out the window. The shade ripped and he plunged to his death. James Forrestal had become one of the first victims of the extraterrestrial cover up, but Forrestal would not be the last... A former CIA agent named Whitey Strieber and the CIA reportedly kept diaries in the White House for several years Strieber later wrote a fictional version diary of Forrestal s diaries and called it Majestic. Then in 1953 a new president occupied the White House. The new president was General of the Army Dwight David Eisenhower. Then in 1953 ten more crashed disc were recovered along with 26 dead and four live aliens four were found in Arizona, two in Texas one in New Mexico one in Louisiana one in Montana one in South Africa. Eisenhower knew he had to beat the alien problem, but he chose not to reveal the secret to Congress yet. Early in 1953 Eisenhower turned to his friend and fellow member in the castle of Foreign Relations, Nelson Rockefeller. Together the two men began planning a secret scripture foreign alien task supervision MJ 12 was thus born.

In 1953 astronomers discovered large objects in space that we're tracking towards the earth evidence proved that the objects can only be space 5 spaceship alien radio communication was intercepted there were several huge ships, and the arrangements were made for the meeting in the desert. An alien hostage was left with the US as a pledge that they would return and formalize a treaty the treaty agreed that bases would be constructed underground for the use of the alienation and the two bases over the treaty agreed that the bases would be constructed underground for the use of the alien nation and the two bases would be constructed for the joint use of the alienation and the United States government. Exchange of technology would take place and they jointly occupied bases. Today all Alien bases are under complete control of the United States Naval Department, only if they are within the United States. It seems that aliens are still found on other planets, and they also have bases that are in some oceans of the world. In his 1980s term, President Ronald Reagan and the Soviet President

Gorbachev agreed to a little-known friendly arrangement. That agreement stated If there is a threat to the world from some species from another planet, we will forget all the little local differences that we have had between our two countries, and we will find out that we're all human beings on this earth. Today the main world problem is the family divider Satan, who began before he tempted Adam and Eve in the garden. Satan and fallen angels begin trying to corrupt the image of man by interbreeding fallen angels with women on the earth as well as mixing the DNA of various creatures and insects with other humans heard most of the so-called extraterrestrials were created from these unions with animals, humans and various insects. Satan had a plan on using the mixed extraterrestrial so that he could continue distributing them throughout the world. This plan had truly begun 1000 years ago, with our world government truly learning from the Adolf Hitler regime who had a relationship with Satan and the aliens. After World War 2, Germans began molding themselves into the US government more than 65 years ago. Various religions began taking note of the secrecy of the extraterrestrials that were that were being covered by that period. The Holy Bible was being understood that Satan's end time plan was to flood earth with so-called aliens.

Satan's plan is to disrupt Jesus' Rapture of The Church. Jesus warns us that many will come falsely in His Name. For the last 65 years, many have died after trying to expose the alien secret. After having my born-again experience in 2011, I told God that I wanted to be one of His best soldiers whatever it took. I had a portal that opened underneath my property, and Satan with other evil creatures and beasts were present in all varieties. I quickly became targeted by the deep state protection operation, which even included a large Indian tobacco growers' group. My life was endangered day and night to my home 100 miles away. My vehicles were nightly being electronically shut down from overhead drones. Frequently ugly aliens were climbing all over my car or truck trying to get into my vehicle. It always happened on the loneliest stretches of roads. That was in Oklahoma, other nights in Missouri would have men on motorcycles chasing me while firing guns at me. Sometimes that was on Interstate I-44 and other times on Hwy. 71 then on Oklahoma Highway 43 those multiple drivers would also try to run me off the road.

Often there would be several vehicles chasing me at the same time. In 2013, one of alien protection criminals killed my youngest daughter who was a senior in college. She had nothing to do with my business Just as the Angel promised me in June 2011, God would never forsake me, and He would do more than I would ever ask of Him That same evening I saw my daughter celebrating in Heaven with both of her Grandmothers That was less than 15 hours after we were notified of her death.

My radio alarm that morning had been set for 7 AM as it usually was on days that I stayed overnight at my business in Southwest Missouri. A Joplin radio announcer had just begun the morning newscast, when he was interrupted by a special severe weather bulletin. The National Weather Service Forecast Office in Norman, Oklahoma, was predicting a highly likely tornado threat over Southeast Kansas and Southwest Missouri by late afternoon. In this part of the Midwest, tornado alerts are so often issued that many times they are not always given the proper attention. I had no idea how accurate that alert would become by the time I got off from work. I got out of bed and went up to the front office to turn on the coffee maker. I then went through the store lobby and unlocked the front doors, and Sheba my Rottweiler excitedly bounded out into the parking lot. That beautiful quiet Sunday morning gave no hint of the deadly weather conditions that were going to develop by late afternoon. I had worked the Saturday afternoon and evening shift from four until midnight at my adult business east of Joplin, Missouri. Since I lived in northeast Oklahoma more than an hour southwest, it was not uncommon for me to stay overnight and open the next morning. I had earlier employed two women who were sister-in-laws, and they had been operating the store for the two shifts each day. One of them moved away so I only had one full time employee, and that required me to start spending much of my life at the business. That afternoon my employee C was coming in at 5 PM, and Sheba and I planned to start home at that time.

I had no inkling, but I was about to experience a most unbelievable rendezvous with destiny on my drive home, that would most positively change my life forever. However, it would be precisely another month before I would learn why such highly unusual and unbelievable things had begun happening to me. On June 25, 2011, I was going to be formally notified by a most eloquent messenger of God that; "God needed me to do something for Him, because of some ability that I had." God wasn't just going to just simply intervene in my life; He would send a real live *angel* in person to make that announcement to me. At sixty-five years of age, I couldn't understand why God would now need me for something, when in fact I had pretty much left Him out of all my adult life. Yet, during all the years when I was not even acknowledging Him, He was still doing great things in my life. It would still be more than two and one-half years, before I would fully understand the reason why God had intervened in my life in 2011. I would begin a gradual learning process on the day that the *angel* delivered the message to me, but it would become a long, amazing journey to the end. That journey is continuing in my life, and it has been twelve years already. From the start it would be almost everyday lessons, where I would face increasingly more powerful enemies. My journey that began on May 22, 2011, would so often remind me of a video game called Dragon Warrior, which I had played with my son many years earlier. In that game, a player graduated up to another world, only after he had defeated the enemy at the end of the previous world. The enemy in each successive world became increasingly more powerful until you got to the last dragon. I was slowly being molded by God into the person that he intended me to become, while He was slowly and methodically pitting me against more difficult challenges. At the time I didn't realize it, but I would no longer have total free will in my life after I was visited by the *angel* on Saturday June 25, 2011. Beginning in August, I would almost daily or nightly be facing real enemies who were spiritually supernatural, and just as powerful as those in the science fiction movies. However, God would be with me every step of the way, and He would always promise me as much strength as I needed against each of them.

As that Sunday progressed at the store, customers coming in were telling me of hearing severe weather bulletins throughout the day. Around 3 PM, I turned finally to The Weather Channel for the best update. Sure enough, there was a large descriptive map on the screen, showing Joplin, Missouri in the bulls- eye for multiple tornadoes. Experts were saying that on The Weather Channel's Tor-Con Scale, there was an eight out of 10 chance that possibly several powerful tornadoes would hit within a 50-mile radius of Joplin by late afternoon. My wife called to remind me that I had left my cell phone charger in my car at home. I was in my truck that weekend and had no portable charger in my truck. I promised my wife that I would use my wall charger for my cell before leaving the store. However, I never got my cell phone charged that day, and it would prove to be a serious mistake. At 5 PM my employee C got in and was telling me that the tornado watches were about to become elevated to warnings. The first actual warnings and sirens for Joplin came at 5:17 PM, and the first touchdown in Joplin would come 15 minutes later.

Finally, at 5:20 Sheba and I were able to leave the store, as the first actual tornado warnings had just been issued, with sirens going off all around the Joplin area. The warning was being broadcast throughout southwest Missouri, southeast Kansas and northeast Oklahoma. As I started my truck, the Joplin radio station was warning the listeners that a very powerful tornado was about to strike Joplin. Then as I started pulling off, C came running out to my truck to tell me that my wife had called to make sure that I got my cell phone charged. Again, I ignored her reminder without going back into the building to charge the phone. I knew that the weather was getting worse fast, and I mistakenly didn't want to take the time. As I drove onto I 44 heading west towards Joplin, the rain was starting to come down very hard, as hard as I had ever seen. The Joplin radio announcer was repeatedly screaming that the tornado sirens were going off and that a tornado touchdown was eminent. I had no idea what to do since I didn't have a tornado shelter at my business anyway. With only my radio and my instincts to guide me, I decided to take a chance on making it to the Fort Smith 71 South Exit and then driving south. In hindsight, I should have gone back inside the store and charged my cell, and I would have allowed a few minutes before leaving the store. Instead, as it was, I was heading straight toward my rendezvous with destiny, and it was less than 20 miles away. As I drove the eight miles to the Kansas City 71 North Exit, the rain was by then getting so hard that my wipers couldn't keep up. After going another 4 or 5 miles, the rain then changed over completely into large hailstones that sounded like bullets hitting my truck. It also became obvious that the wind gusts were getting stronger the further west I drove. The hailstones had begun at about the size of golf balls but now I could see that they were quickly increasing in size and intensity. I was now only about 5 miles east of the Fort Smith Exit where I had planned to exit off onto Highway 71 South. My plan was that if it seemed possible when I got off at the 71 South Exit, I would be going straight south and slightly perpendicular to the tornado path that was being reported on the radio. There were now monstrous amounts of large hail coming down and I have never seen or heard of anything like what I witnessed next. The massive amounts of hail that was falling began changing into cylindrical shapes, and they appeared as if in chutes each individually the diameter of a 5-gallon bucket. It looked and sounded as if there were 100-pound bags of ice chunks crashing down all over my truck. At that point, I fully expected my hood and roof to collapse any second along with my entire windshield. Over the period of the next several weeks, I talked with two different over the road truck drivers, who had experienced the same hailstone phenomena near Joplin that afternoon. They both agreed that they had never seen anything near to the size and intensity of that hail. I had always believed that the hail intensity correlated to the strength of an accompanying tornado, and it certainly was true that afternoon. I grabbed my cell phone and tried to reach my wife and quickly to tell her that I was almost in the tornado. She answered, and I said, "I am in the tornado" and as I started to tell her that I loved her, my cell phone went dead. I was then approaching Fort Smith 71 South Exit. The overpass just east of that exit was packed with vehicles, as was the interstate up ahead of me. People who could not decide what they should do were haphazardly trying to turn around and go back east, but they couldn't drive across the median. There were hordes of vehicles simply stopping in the middle of the interstate and many were stuck within the median. Then several hundred yards further up west of the exit ramp, I watched a small white pickup come flying across the interstate and it looked to be up 50 feet in the air. That truck sailed over the north side of the interstate and went completely out of my sight.

That truck was only the first flying vehicle that I saw, but then there seemed to be a wave of several flying over the highway in different places all at once. Two of those vehicles were up 100 feet or more above the highway and they looked as if they landed more than 100 yards north of the interstate. I knew that there had to be lots of people dying at that interchange, because of the way cars and semi-trucks were lying upside down in every direction. The highway and on both sides of the median appeared to be littered with equipment of every kind. I could now determine that wall to wall vehicles were blocking the southbound exit which I had intended to take, and that numerous autos and semis were also jammed into both lanes of the highway. That logjam of vehicles which kept me from continuing west on I-44, most likely saved my life that afternoon. I hurriedly pulled off the interstate less than 50 feet from the southbound exit ramp and wormed my way off the roads edge. I eased on to the downwind side of a tractor trailer rig which had Texas license plates. As I parked on the north side of that truck, I knew that I would never forget it, because it was an orange tractor transporting a red trailer. I had stopped directly north of the Flying J Truck Terminal, but I was on the opposite side of I-44. Since I was parked right at the rear of the trailer, I had a clear unobstructed view of the entire truck terminal and parking lot. My initial thoughts were that the orange and red tractor trailer would possibly flip over onto my truck. I realized that possibility when I was forced to park in that position, but there was no other way to park and no other place to move to. As I looked south directly over the interstate, it seemed as if the entire truck terminal and everything around it was leaving the ground. I vividly remember a unique feeling of total calmness that came over me, as I watched the air becoming filled with debris of all kinds flying towards me. The first tornado damage to the vehicles on the interstate happened as I was approaching, and I never felt that wind anymore after I got parked. It seemed that the first wave of the tornado had come across the interstate just west of the exit ramp. If the road had not been blocked ahead of me, I would have driven right past the clogged ramp directly into where the deadliest part of the tornado was about to cross.

As if by God's own hand, the windblown debris that was flying directly toward me instantly stopped and very slowly lifted everything above the interstate just before it crossed it. I never felt anything, as the massive wall of assorted debris began floating overhead my truck. As the debris lifted above and over the interstate, it appeared that it began moving in a very slow motion, and it all seemed to be floating within a vivid Pea Green colored band that was also drifting so slowly to the northeast. The debris mass appeared to be moving slower as it was all seemingly floating right above my truck. I sensed then that Sheba was slowly moving over towards me, and she gently laid her head in my lap. The Joplin radio station was on, and the announcer was screaming at how horrific the damage was in Joplin and was tearfully describing everything that he was seeing. He obviously had grown up in Joplin and was hurting badly as he identified specific damaged locations. As I began looking around, I was also seeing terrible carnage in every direction. My location was about 3 miles southeast as the crow flies, from the Range line area of Joplin where that reporter was. Of course, he was only seeing the Range Line Road commercial area, and there would be far more damage west of Range line. As I watched thousands of objects slowly drifting overhead in the Pea Green Belt, I remember saying out loud "it must have hit a big clothing store. "I was seeing a flood of shirts, pants, dresses, hats etc. floating along overhead, and all of it was in the slow-moving wave of Pea Green background. I was acquainted with a couple who owned an EMT business in an adjoining county, who came into my store sometimes. I learned from them several weeks later that only torsos and less were what most of the recovered body parts had consisted of. That graphically explained why I mistakenly thought I was seeing items out of a damaged clothing store, and I could also see masses of large objects including large animals and such, that were floating along as well. Just as Sheba slowly lowered her head onto my lap, I felt that I was going to go to sleep as well. The very last thing that I heard as I was "going to sleep" was the radio announcer screaming that the Wal-Mart off Range line had been destroyed. I had not turned off my truck or the radio when "we went to sleep." On Monday, the day after the tornado, a flood of memories began coming back to me. I clearly remembered that I had said out loud, as I I was being mesmerized by the slow movement overhead, "hey were dead, but this isn't bad." At that moment I felt an indescribable peace, which I have never felt before or since in my life. Yet it seemed that just after saying, "I'm dead", I began hearing two Joplin radio announcers on the air, and one of them was saying "well it is now 6:35 PM and a little over an hour since it hit." At the exact same moment, the orange semi next to me revved his engine as he began pulling out onto the interstate. Right at that point, I knew by the time lapse that me and my dog Sheba had been "dead" for nearly an hour. My truck had been idling during the entire time and the radio had been on as well, because all I had to do was put my truck in gear and drive out behind the semi. Clearly without a doubt, as the first radio announcer began describing all the destruction that he was witnessing, Sheba and I were about to temporarily pass into the spirit world. Then when I heard the two radio announcers and the semi start up, I knew that we were no longer dead; and it immediately felt like a ton of weight had dropped back onto my shoulders. At that same instant, Sheba slowly raised her body up and began looking around. I have relived in my mind that entire incident hundreds of times, and there is no doubt that we were allowed to live for nearly an hour in totally spiritual bodies. I obviously didn't know it at that time, but as the rest of my journey unfolded, I would understand, that God had enabled us to do that for a distinct purpose. I would soon learn that God had planned it, so that I would be able to understand and function in that spiritual world. I would need to understand it better, because I was soon going to be literally living in parallel worlds simultaneously. My functioning pretty much 24/7 in dual worlds was going to last almost two years. God would provide me more than two months of awesome spiritual training constantly surrounded night and day by mostly friendly spirits. Then beginning in early August, I would have to adapt to living in a world that began teeming with evil supernatural extraterrestrials. It is important to know that I never had any feeling of impending doom that afternoon, even as the tornado debris appeared to be heading towards us. It was a fact that the wind and rain had abruptly stopped just as the tornado lifted and floated above the interstate. There is no doubt that the flying debris lifting over I-44 at that point saved the lives of us and countless others. God had clearly shown me in super slow motion that He and Only He had purposely saved my physical body from death that day. Also, I would soon learn that my spiritual body had been saved from the eternal fire of Hell. Had I died that day;

I would have entered directly into Hell. I had no earthly idea that afternoon as I drove away, that Jesus Christ had appeared and saved me. He had also taken me into the spiritual dimension for nearly an hour, and my life was being changed forever.

As the tornado passed, I began worrying about whether my home and wife in Oklahoma had survived. Since I had no way to contact her, I began trying to weave my way through the debris onto Highway 71 South toward my home 30 miles away. I saw less wind damage as I drove further south away from the interstate, and by the time I got to Seneca, Missouri there was no sign of any damage. I drove southwesterly the remaining 12 miles into Oklahoma and as I drove into my farm, I saw that all my barns were intact. My wife came outside as I drove up to the house and she was standing on the back deck. The massive tornado, which had created such horrific destruction and had claimed thousands of lives, had totally missed my farm.

I never even later had any dreams or nightmares of the occurrences of that day. However, the next afternoon I found myself in deep thought about two things specifically that had happened to us. One was the apparent fact that me and my beloved dog had been allowed to enter the spirit world for almost an hour. I knew that we were feeling no impending doom when it happened, so why did that happen? Then another vivid memory that came back to me as I was standing in the Seneca, Missouri post office waiting to mail a package. I had one vivid intriguing display that I had been shown while in the spirit world, and I now believe that God intended for me to understand. It was a scene that has never stopped coming back to me sometimes daily, even after 12 years have passed. That scene was of me floating above a very large flat table or game board that was set up in a massive airplane hangar. The hangar had the feeling of being on a military base somewhere. There were many people standing around one side of that table, but I could see no gender or description of any of those people. The table appeared as that of a very large, illustrated game board, which had several dark grey round game pieces stacked on one end of the table. Then as I looked down upon the flat game table, at least three of the "game pieces" one at a time, quickly slid down the table and flew off the game board. I could clearly identify the familiar weather depiction of a tornado Vortex inscribed on each of the sliding objects. They each seemed to slide along the table right underneath where I was floating, before flying off the end of the table. I had once won some money in a slot machine jackpot in an Oklahoma casino, and that casino game was called Vortex. It had a large picture of that dark grey tornado vortex on the top of the machine. Those game pieces were individual vortexes looking exactly as the ones used in hurricane and tornado scenarios on weather maps. It was several days later when I began hearing that the Joplin Tornado had multiple vortexes. I will allow everyone to each make their own assumption as to what my vision represented, but my feeling that afternoon in the post office was the following and still is to this day. In 2011 our government had an active program called HAARP or High Frequency Active Auroral Research Program, which among the many capabilities had the capacity to create severe weather conditions anywhere in the world. It can be checked out online at HAARP. Several highly educated individuals have called it a Pandora's Box. More than two months later, I would be told by a well-qualified individual that in fact a very real Portal had opened on my property at Exit 26 in Reeds, Missouri. He would also confirm that the Portal had opened immediately after the Joplin Tornado, and that I had unknowingly been seeing it nightly since June. The timing and the location of the Portal opening would make me understand, that God was also using it for His Purposes with many of the tornado victims. The Portal was being used as well for the Biblical teachings, which God was presenting to us in my building day and night. However, I would also become well informed of the evil ramifications of that shortcut to our world from another dimension. Albert Einstein had once theorized in a summation of dimensional openings, that they could well be a good side - bad side experiment. Einstein explained simply, that if we opened doorways into other worlds, unknown evil could enter our world at the same time. One of my questions will always be, was the Joplin Tornado coincidental to the Portal opening at that time? I ask that question now because it became quite evident, that a top-secret branch of our government began utilizing the Portal location on my property very shortly after the tornado. Their operations began quickly with every night operations within two months after the deadly tornado. Their arrogant illegal takeover of my property would officially begin on August 6, 2011, and would greatly damage my business operation, my employees, and every facet of my life. It would flood evil extraterrestrial entities in and out of the portal, the home behind my business, and into all my vehicles. I would every day and night be driving, with some variety of bastards and reprobates in my autos, Reprobates is God's Word for all those evil creatures. Most of the extraterrestrial creatures that would be unloaded every night into my automobiles and buildings, would be humans cloned with numerous varieties of non-human entities. I would be most fortunate whenever a stranger, with valuable insight into what was taking place, appeared at my business shortly after the creatures began coming into my property through the Portal. That former longtime government employee would in detail, explain to me the dangerous ramifications of my exposing that operation. His knowledge had been gained through years of service within a similar top-secret agency. He would warn me of a specific government organization, and the seriousness of the threats that I was about to face, because of my intent to expose the alien run cloning program. He would also identify certain a local individual Joplin relative who had already targeted me. That visitor would be another of God's Angels who would appear in my life at that time, and I took his warnings seriously. I would begin documenting his information with others in the event something should happen to me.

The next day after the tornado was Monday May 23, 2011, and by afternoon I found myself going over and over in my mind about those two happenings during the tornado. Yet by Wednesday of that week, I was back to my old self. The only difference that I could see in myself was that it seemed I may be having a little more patience with people in my life. That would later prove to be an early indication of the man who I was intended to eventually become. Impatience and intolerance with others had always been two of my worst traits, so more patience would be welcomed by everyone.

On Thursday, May 26, I left for the afternoon work in Sarcoxie at 4 PM. Around the entire business property area we had a total of 17 motion activated cameras inside and out. Inside the 2800 ft. building there were 9 cameras, and there were an additional 8 of the same type cameras covering the large parking lot and the exterior of the building. This was now the fourth day since the tornado on Sunday. At around 8:30 PM, I was alone in the store. It was always my habit to constantly pay attention to the cameras that were being activated by outside movements. I saw movement on three of the fronts outside cams and it appeared that multiple dark Blue vertical lines were moving from west to east across the front parking lot. I knew it was like nothing that I had seen before but thought it may be a technical problem. As the night went on, the blue lines became more pronounced as they moved across the parking lot from the west to the east. Just before I closed at midnight, it occurred to me that these lines must be people in spirit form. Yet they were all still only blue lines with mechanical like movements. I drove home that night after closing and mentioned the lines to my wife. She said it was likely something in the camera connections, and not people. The next day was Friday, May 27, and I didn't get into work until 4 PM. I had a busy day as usual, Friday afternoon and evening, with the blue lines still very evident. C, my day employee, had still not seen them at all. I had not mentioned it to her yet either since I didn't want a bunch of unnecessary rumors out. Shortly after 6 PM on Friday, the blue lines appeared and quickly changed into human forms. They were clearly human males and appeared as in the18 to 25-year-old range. They were all dressed in outfits that were either light green, light blue or light red respectively. Their clothing all appeared to be the exact same type outfits, of pants, work boots, and short-sleeved hospital type shirts, with two top pockets. The young men were marching single file in lines around the front parking lot. I had an immediate discernment of evil from them by their erect unpleasant facial expressions, and later I would be proven correct in my initial assessment of them. They had appeared in the west parking lot and began then walking to the east, which took them directly in front of the store. Additionally, I would also witness many hundreds of times when evil entities of all varieties would come from the west parking area. We always observed that good entities of every kind would come from the east, and I would later learn that the East is synonymous with the direction from which Jesus will return to this Earth. Sheba and I got up and walked outside and we could both clearly see the marching entities, but they appeared as if they saw neither of us. I watched intently then as two customer cars were driving into the front parking lot up to the store. As each person exited their car, it was obvious that they were not seeing the spirits and were walking right next to them. However, I realized the fact that I could see the spirits, almost guaranteed that there would be a few other people who could see them also. I knew that those entities merely being there would not be something that would help the business either way. I stayed overnight on Friday at the store, because I wanted to see if they stayed around all night in the parking lot. I had a feeling that they may leave after I closed the store at midnight. After I closed, I stayed in my back office for a couple of hours taking care of some paperwork. The spirits showed no sign of leaving the parking lot as of 2AM, when we went to bed. The next morning Saturday May 28, Sheba and I were out of bed an hour earlier than usual. I went up front to let Sheba out and to start some coffee, and it was just barely 6 AM. The first thing that I noticed on the monitors was, that there were even more entities in the parking lot now, than there were when we went to bed. I decided to thaw a frozen breakfast that I had in the freezer. By the time the food was thawed and cooked it was nearly 7:00 AM, and the entities had finally begun disappearing. I still didn't plan to tell anyone except my wife what was going on there. She was more than an hour away in Oklahoma and still had not seen any of the evidence, but it was obvious that she didn't believe me as to anything that I was seeing. Her contentions were that I was suffering hallucinations due to the tornado experience a week earlier. Later she would begin telling people, including my employee, that I was hallucinating. The real irony would be that some of my associates, who visited there frequently, would begin seeing the entities themselves. The female employee would be afraid to tell her that she saw them too, even when she finally did see them. Shortly I would begin showing the entities to a few choice customers, as well as some of my trusted associates who visited frequently. The strangest part was that she never wanted to go up and see what was even on the cameras. This was only the tip of the many icebergs that were coming into my life. The one great thing about it was that I was accumulating literally hundreds of pictures, almost every day and night. I was constantly taking pictures with my cell phone, and additionally store cams recorded movement activated pictures 24/7 and saved them. Every time during the workdays or nights that I found time, I would sat down in the office and check the outside cam pictures from last 24 hours. The daily pictures were growing more numerous and intriguing.

Let me say at this point, my life had already been quite colorful. I grew up on a family farm, which was the remaining portion of a once quite large farming plantation north of Tallahassee, Florida. My ancestors, the Moore's and the Lees, were some of the area's first settlers. My Grandfather Thomas Moore and his brother, my

Great Uncle Walter, both fought for the Confederacy during the Civil War. Together in the same unit, they fought in every major battle up the East Coast, all the way to Gettysburg. My great uncle Walter was wounded at Gettysburg and was lying on the battlefield for 24 hours unattended. However, both safely returned to Tallahassee after the war and were productive citizens for many years. They then became responsible for each managing a large portion of the family farming operation that was in two different areas of Leon County, Florida. Their father my great-grandfather, John Moore had died in 1865 just as the Civil War was ending. Neither of the sons was older than 21 years old at that time. Their younger brother Johnny was too young for the Civil War, but he fought in the Spanish American War in Cuba. I also had three greats on my mother's side of the family who each also fought in the Civil War. One of them died in a Union prison camp in Chicago and is buried there today. My great-grandmother Louisa Moore was a Cherokee Indian who was from North Carolina. Her family had been part of a group of slightly more than 600 North Carolina Cherokees, who had avoided the dreadful Trail of Tears March in 1838-39, which was called by the Cherokee, "The Trail Where They Cried." A local merchant named William H. Thomas, who was also a North Carolina Senator, was able to secure North Carolina Citizenship for all the Cherokees in that group. They became forever known as the Eastern Band of the Cherokee, and many of them would join on the side of the Confederacy during the Civil War. Senator William Thomas later became a Colonel in the Confederate Army, and his troops were all members of the Eastern Band of the Cherokee. His fabled unit, which was comprised of mostly Cherokees, fired the last shots of the Civil War in a battle in South Carolina. The horrific Trail of Tears journey to Oklahoma took the lives of an estimated 2,000 of the Cherokees, including the wife of Chief John Ross. John Ross worked hard to try and improve the conditions and survivability of the trail, and he is credited with saving the lives of many by doing so. Sadly, John Ross' own wife Quatre died along that journey and the last words she said to her husband were, "I'll be waiting for you." While living in Oklahoma for more than 15 years, I have learned much about the proud Cherokee people and their struggle. During that time, I have grown so very proud of being a Cherokee descendant of my Great Grandmother. That pride would be bolstered by the many spiritually powerful Cherokee ancestors who would actively appear in my life in late 2011 and in 2012. Precisely in the early morning of August 7, 2011, Cherokee Spirits would appear and begin working on my behalf in unbelievable ways. Three days later, I discovered that my business property adjacent to I-44 and Highway 37 at Reeds, Missouri, adjoined the Cherokee Trail of Tears on two sides where it traversed through southwest Missouri. That punishing thousand-mile march had begun in North Carolina in 1838, and had ended in Tahlequah, Oklahoma. I was informed that the Trail had crossed through the golf course which adjoined my property on the north side. Then the Trail turned south on Missouri Highway 37 on its route to Tahlequah, and Highway 37 ran beside my property on the west side. I was able to learn of that on August 8 after we began witnessing a daily ritual in my parking lot.

During, those days I would begin understanding that the so-called Five Civilized Tribes were then worshipping the same God, which most of us still worship today. I would see and feel many hundreds of awe-inspiring illustrations, of God's Plan for the spiritually powerful Cherokee Spirits who supported me. They would be around me every day and night, and it had begun at 6:30 on the Sunday morning of August 7, 2011. They would be with me through some of the toughest times and would continue through October of 2013 when I would finally close my business. I would begin to feel so much pride in my Cherokee Heritage and I would develop an indescribable bond to the beautiful spirits who surrounded me. They would always make themselves known to me, during those lonely and dangerous times. As a person who used to never cry at anything, I still become emotional remembering the feeling of their presence around me during those times. There were three individual Cherokee braves who would act out funny scenes right outside my front door that always seemed to make me laugh. Those three men would often appear late at night when I had been having an especially bad day. I had one l close associate who would also be allowed to watch during some of those times. That same man became quite familiar with some of the other spiritual demonstrations, including a Tribal Council appearance that happened every day that I was at the store. It would start at 3:30pm daily and it always got my undivided attention, because it contributed much to my morale. The Tribal Council appearances were also often watched by other people who happened to come into the store between 3:30 and 5:30 pm. It never ceased to amaze me, that most could not appreciate the unparalleled mystique of what they were witnessing. Some of the spiritual tribal council protests I was able to get saved on the surveillance logs, but the images came through quite faint, as was expected. I will forever cherish the loyalty of the many Cherokees relatives from long ago, and each will always be vivid in my memory. I humbly pray that by the spiritual demonstration's others can appreciate the countless ways in which our Father shows us his love when we are hurting. There were so many other times when I witnessed the beauty and strength of my Cherokee ancestors, and their dedication to helping me. Throughout the next couple of years, there will be so many more specific instances of their spiritual interactions with me. I was often told by the Delaware Tribal Council that very people living would ever witness the spiritual events that I was able to see.

I grew up with a passion for the outdoors, which I inherited from both sides of my family. I began at a very young age, hunting and fishing along the Ochlocknee River which flowed through parts of our original family land. I was raised in a truly Christian home with evidence of Christian teaching all around me. My dad and mother truly loved God, and they tried very hard to instill strong Christian beliefs in me. However, as I grew up, I seemed to gravitate to older friends to associate with. By the time I was 17 years old my biggest goal in life was spending time with my friends, and not having to get up and attend church every Sunday morning. I was always made to attend church as I was growing up, every Sunday morning and many Sunday nights as well. I grew up in a little country church that was not more than a mile from my home. It was a small Methodist church that my Grandmother Moore had overseen the construction of in honor of my grandfather. He was at that time in his later years of life, but many family members would attend that church for their entire lives. Today, I appreciate how growing up in that cozy little family church has provided me with many beautiful memories of my childhood. I only recently began remembering and appreciating, how my devoted parents had provided me so much spiritual background toward a Christian life. Even after all those years of my Christian childhood, I was still truly saved by God's Grace, which was bestowed upon me in my 65th year of life. I had always felt that I had to come back to the church one day, but had God not sent an angel to me, I would not have made it back. My Dad died when I was 18 years old and was a senior in high school, and I am sure that his last thoughts were of his family. The night that he died on Sunday January 19, 1964, I had just turned 18 and I thought I knew everything. Yet when we left him that night at the hospital, I never understood that he had been trying to prepare us that afternoon for his eminent death. I have always wished I would have hugged his neck and told him goodbye, but I barely remember leaving and it was only two hours later that he died all alone. I knew for a fact that if Heaven was as real as he always told us, that he would certainly be there. I have seen my dad three times since July 9, 2011, and I know for a fact that he is in Paradise, which will be heaven at the end of the Millennium. I also knew that he was quite worried about my outlook on life and afraid of how I would turn out without him.

My Dad was very intelligent and far above his educational years. He was so correct in his worrying about me, because I would certainly choose some treacherous paths in my life. The same night that I graduated from high school in 1965, I left Tallahassee with a friend, and we drove straight through to New York City. We had jobs promised working in the 1964-65 World's Fairs that was being held in Flushing Meadows. That New York experience further fueled an already existing wild adventure mode in me. It opened a world which that small town country boy had never seen, and it set in motion a lifelong search for even greater excitement. Later in life that desire for excitement would lead me to some quite extraordinary opportunities, but with endangerments as well. It seemed that throughout my entire life I tended to encounter some quite bizarre experiences, both good and bad.

From the young age of 12 years old, there were a lot of very close calls in my life, and they all had hit very close to me. One mid-December afternoon in 1958, my uncle and I were hunting on family property, and had no idea that one of my first cousins was in the same big woods. That afternoon, my cousin was mistaken for a deer by my uncle and was shot and killed. I saw and heard the evidence of it that cold Saturday afternoon only one week before Christmas. Two years earlier, one afternoon I was riding in a car with an older neighbor, who was driving his brand new 1956 Ford 120 miles an hour. Two nights later, in that same car, he died in a crash less than a half mile from my house. When I was 20 years old, I wrecked a new sports car, while driving on a curvy country road at a very high speed. The car was totally demolished, and I walked away without a scratch, only within a few days bought another car with an even faster engine in it. Within the next four years after my car crash, I would have five close friends, who would die in automobile accidents due to alcohol and speeding. Another very close friend, who was the best man in my wedding in June 1970, was shot and killed in Miami Florida. He was killed by a teenager at a traffic light in Miami Florida, early morning on Christmas Eve 1970. It was almost exactly 6 months after my wedding that he died needlessly. That was a total of eight people who were close in my life, who had died in tragic alcohol related accidents within a few short years. In all the incidents, I had very close associations in some manner with each.

I grew up in Tallahassee and attended high school and college there. My wife and I had married in 1970 and we owned a couple of businesses there for a lot of years. We also had three beautiful children who were born in Tallahassee. In 1983, there came a time when I became employed in a Presidential Ordered Special National Defense Program. I was one of two CIA Covert Operatives scheduled for a mission into a communist country. That was during the latter days of the Cold War which had smoldered for many years between the United States and the former Soviet Union. In March 1983, President Ronald Reagan made a speech calling The Soviet Union the Evil Empire. Within three weeks, my partner and I began working in a quite volatile high stakes environment. Whenever we left the country, we were reminded that we may be killed or captured and that if either situation occurred, our government would not be able even confirm our existence. My partner and I had both been profiled as ones who were most comfortable operating on the "thin line between life and death. "Maybe they were correct about that assessment and were likely related to our lifetime penchants for high adventure. My partner and I eventually were delivered an appreciative tribute from then President Ronald Reagan for our most successful mission. After our work, we received a quite lucrative book proposal from a top New York Publishing Agent. The offer was for us permitting our factual story of involvement in specific non-classified government operations that had been completed. The intended author Arnaud De Borchgrave was an international writer of fiction espionage novels and was an acquaintance of the then current CIA Director. The author had recently published an international bestseller in fiction account of a quite similar scenario, so we were told to be prepared for a movie deal as well. We were a couple of days away from the meeting in New York, when the then CIA Director Casey decided that he had changed his mind and he didn't want the story to be told at that time. We appreciated Mr. Casey's concerns at that time as well. To this day the real story behind the success of our mission has never been revealed. President Reagan's personal tribute commended us in his message; for our work involving what he referred to as the single most important national defense objective of his presidency. Without disclosing specific details, it was mainly due to the foresight and resolve of President Reagan that his long-term objective had been successful. Few have ever known that the President's objective had been successful to a level where the Soviets had thrown in the towel, they had unofficially surrendered to the United States. The Berlin Wall had voluntarily been torn down and the Soviet Union had agreed to several breakups of the country and their military had been severely weakened. Some 18 years later all those years of dedication and work by so many would seem to be for naught. It is my belief that President Ronald Reagan was one of the greatest leaders that this country ever had. Today, it is a well-established fact that in the last six and one-half years the current presidential administration has dribbled away a priceless accomplishment which was first achieved under the Reagan -Bush Administration. Much of that accomplishment had been well maintained and even strengthened throughout the subsequent Bush 41 and 43 Administrations. The enemy had been dramatically weakened by our mutually strong military and diplomatic measures during those three administrations. However, beginning in 2009, our enemies were allowed to rebuild while our military was being held back. The best military that the world has ever known was restrained from doing what they have always done best. Biblical Prophecy is quickly being fulfilled these days precisely as promised. I believe that some of our leaders will receive their just reward from God for their actions. We have witnessed the forced demoralization of the fabric of our society, and it is a sad day for our country.

On Monday March 3, 1999, my family was within several months of moving from Alabama to Southern Oklahoma. We had an F-1 tornado that night, which developed suddenly out of a severe thunderstorm. The tornado had formed over a small lake next to our home, and within three minutes it hit our house and destroyed a good portion of it. If the tornado had lasted longer, it would have done far more damage. While that tornado was not near as powerful as the Joplin tornado, it still was a quite painful experience. I mention all these experiences, only to reflect that I have endured many tough situations and have never succumbed to any hallucinations or paranoid delusions. So it became quite disturbing when I found that my wife was telling my family and others, that I was suffering from delusions and hallucinations. As the story progressed, it would finally become evident who was behind the accusations of my having a mental illness. I had witnessed many pretty gruesome things in my life, but unfortunately, they had all been real. I would encounter many evil as well as beautiful things in the months ahead, and they all would be 100% real. To my wife, the blue lines that I was seeing were evidence of hallucinations of some sort. Now I was about to tell her that the lines were human spirit. Considering this new revelation last night, I decided to call my employee C and let her have off all weekend until Monday morning. This meant that I would stay over at the store all weekend, and I would close at midnight on Sunday, May 29. Now I was anxious to see if this group of spirits would show up again tonight. Saturday, moved along busily as most Saturdays did. I had gotten involved in the usual chores of the day, and it was already 7 PM. Since it had passed the time that the spirits usually showed in the evening, I was watching the cameras with much interest. At 8 PM I had still seen no spirits in the parking lot. The phone rang and it was a former employee relative calling, she and her aunt are coming by to bring me a Subway. I had a refrigerator, microwave, and food, but had not eaten yet so her offer was accepted. They got to my place near 8:30 PM, and we ate sandwiches and visited a bit. Still no sign of any spirits and it was right now at 9 PM. suddenly the male spirits began showing up on the front cameras, it was a Saturday night, and they were in rare form. I had no idea yet, but what I will later refer to as God's Crash Course on Spirits, had officially begun. I would begin learning many things, which are not known to us in our flesh bodies in this life. My friends and I were sitting in my office behind the front counter. All of my inside and outside cameras were monitored in my office, as well as at the counter. Simultaneously S and her aunt screamed out, Lynwood, those are ghosts at the front door. As I tried to make a feeble joke that it wasn't what it looked like, the camera at the west door was showing more spirits standing beside that door, as well. I continued trying to play it all down, but the spirits would have no part of it. They began hitting the building at the front door and side door at the same time. At that point, I had no choice but to admit to them, that, yes it was all real. S and her aunt both knew that I had been near the tornado. So I began explaining to them how things had happened since then, with the spirits. I also told them how I was not believed by my wife. It sounded so strange saying that to them, as we're sitting there watching these entities in both areas of the parking lot. S, whose ex in-law had worked for me several years ago, I had known for a long time. She was a good person and truly cared about others. She got up and went out to her car, and came back with a 4-inch tall, very old gray colored metal cross on a chain. On it was engraved With God All Things Are Possible. The cross had belonged to her recently deceased favorite grandmother, and I could tell that it meant a lot to her. Even though neither she nor I had that much of a close relationship with God, I still very much appreciated that gift. Throughout the next several years, that cross would be with me during many unbelievably tough situations as well as beautiful ones. I have that little cross to this day and it serves to remind me of where I began four long unbelievable years ago.

<hr>

On Sunday, May 29, it had now been one week since the deadly tornado, and Joplin. I had witnessed a week of very bizarre things happening. Yet very few people knew that it was happening, so far. I wondered at this point, why none of the spirits were actually inside the building. My question will be answered within the next week, in a big way. On Monday, May 30 through Thursday, June 9, 2011, were pretty much the same happenings every night. If I didn't work one night, none of the spirits would appear on any of the outside cameras. So far C, my employee had seen nothing, but I had now told her about the spirits. I went into work on Thursday at 5 PM, and I planned to stay over the weekend until Sunday evening. C was going to be off until Sunday afternoon when she would come in. I closed around midnight and Sheba, and I went to sleep. When we awoke at 7 AM Friday morning, the entities disappeared as the sun came up, like they usually did. That Friday morning was the 10th of June, and my wife called at 11:45 AM, to tell me that our little 11-year-old dog Dingo had been run over and killed by a meter reader. Dingo was a very special little dog, which we had found trapped in the top of an uncapped oil well in Southern Oklahoma in the year 2000. I named him Dingo because he looked like one of the wild dogs of Africa. When we lived in southern Oklahoma, I ran close to 500 head of cattle throughout much of the year, and anytime I went out night or day, Dingo was always with me. He loved to sit in a chair on our porch there, and bark at things coming around. When I fried chicken wings outside, he liked to catch chicken skins, that I would pitch to him. The meter reader for the utility company was driving carelessly coming into the farm; otherwise, he would have never run over Dingo. My wife had him cremated and we have his remains still. The rest of the day Friday was kind of sad because of me losing my little dog. As I closed that evening, there seemed to be a lot more entities in my parking lot. It had rained throughout most of the night and was slowly clearing just after daylight. It was little after 7 AM, and Sheba and I were behind the store counter, and had not unlocked the main door yet. Since it had been raining all night, the sun was slower coming through the clouds. I unlocked the main door, propped it open and Sheba went outside into the parking lot. Several minutes later, she came back into the store through the open front door. I got myself a cup of coffee and sat down directly in front of the main camera monitor. The overnight rain had slowed to just a very light sprinkle, and the sun was sparkling like diamonds, through the raindrops. Suddenly, I saw a line of entities coming around the corner of the building, from the west side parking lot. Then instantly, at the front door a large black bobtail dog on a leash appeared, and he was staring right into the main camera. I was trying to imagine what was happening when the dog walked forward, and then I saw that his leash was being held by a tall evil entity in a light-yellow outfit. It was just like a dog show as then the next dog walked forward and stopped directly in front of the door as the first had. I said out loud "that's Dingo", and at that my little Dingo stared directly into the camera, wagging his tail with that excited happy look. He stood there looking as real as he ever had been then walked forward as his handler followed just as the first dog had done. All I could think about was that it was just like a dog show. Then a mass of tall male entities, in red, yellow and blue garments, began pouring in through the front door, that I had left open. Sheba was standing up with her front feet on the counter, watching them just as I was. I totally didn't know what to make of this new happening, but it wouldn't be long until I found out. We could see every one of them as they were within 5 feet of the counter, and they disappeared into different areas of the building. Now they had truly moved inside of the building for the first time.

Now another most strange thing had happened, and once more I was feeling total disbelief. I thought about it for a few minutes and decided to call my wife and tell her about it. Of course, she didn't believe this at all either, for I knew I had a really strange situation developing in my life. She then told me that I needed to get some mental help badly, because the tornado had caused PTSD in me. To say that I was greatly agitated, is putting it too mildly. After 40 years of marriage, we had developed tons of trust in each other. We knew that we could rely on each other for support, no matter how tough something was. I was witnessing the beginning of the most painful thing that had ever happened in my entire life. That pain was to grow many times worse, over the next several years. We had three children that were in their mid to late 20s, and we were very close to them emotionally. This disbelief by my wife would have ramifications that would reverberate into every facet of our family life. I discovered that my three children were already being told that I had suffered mental trauma from the tornado, and that I was refusing to get help. Ironically, our oldest daughter was the Director of a state mental treatment facility in Alabama. Since she was 750 miles away, she was relying totally on her mother's disinformation about, of all things, her father's delusions and hallucinations. My other two children lived in Oklahoma, in Tulsa, my son was 28 and my daughter was 25. My son also had a degree, and my youngest daughter was one year away from her senior year at OU. Let me say at this point, that my children knew well that I had always had a clear sound mind. I was always the problem solver in the family, whether it was their problems or someone else's, I was always the one to get the problems resolved. I had always faced tough things head-on, just as I would have to face this coming battle alone, but it would hurt me beyond anyone's comprehension. As the story got much meaner, that distrust would likely prevent me from being able to save my youngest daughter's life. I was the one who knew better than anyone how wild it was becoming, but I had to stay with it even though I sometimes only had the help of some almost strangers. Some of my enemies would be supernatural and invisible much of the time, while others would be politically connected, cowardly criminals. The equalizer though would be my Heavenly Father, and when things would become the toughest, God would produce His most awesome miracles before my eyes. It would be during those times that He would teach me faith, in ways that are difficult for non-believers to understand. He would send unknown strangers to help me along the way, but ultimately it would be God, my two loyal intelligent dogs and me. God was preparing me for progressively tougher enemies, and he ultimately would introduce me up close, to the Prince of Darkness. Without knowing it I alone would be in the physical Presence of God, when I calmly asked Him a question. God in His strong clear voice would immediately answer my question, and it would happen in my office at 3:00 in the morning on September 17, 2011. That morning for four straight hours, I would be present during a battle that represented the Fifth Trump and part of the Sixth in the Book of Revelations, which is the Final Chapter of the Bible. God's indescribable gift to me, would guarantee that I would forever be a most pro- active soldier in God's Army. I would clearly be shown that every single person living in this world is now living in the last few years of Biblical Prophecy. These are the times that all the famous prophets in the Bible wanted to be living in.

I wasn't going to abandon my business and there was nothing else to do but deal with it. I've never lacked self-confidence in my life and knowing that my mental state was fine, I was going to deal with it. I was beginning to realize that my temporarily dying during the tornado was directly tied to what was happening. The one comforting thing in the entire ordeal was that I had several close associates who looked at the camera images regularly and saw what I saw. Some of them could also see the actual entities in the parking lot as well as those in the truck and cars. Anyone could see the images that were appearing in the cameras, because I had learned that regular ghosts can't hide from cameras, mirrors, or shadows. Though I would learn beginning on August 6, 2011, that most entities from other worlds can hide from cameras. I was thinking that I had better start handling most of the night shifts, since so far the spirits that only showed up between dark and shortly after daylight. I didn't know what was going to happen, but I knew that I needed to keep control in my hands as much as possible. I've been in a lot of tough situations and always found a way to get through to him. I never would have walked out if I could have, and it hadn't really gotten bad yet.

I decided I would take Sheba and drive the 3 miles to the convenience store, after I closed that night. I had begun seeing the spirits inside the store off and on that night, and I could see them at times near some of the customers. I didn't see anyone that night who acted like they saw anything, but I knew some people would be able to see them and that was another stressor for me to deal with. I now understood that for whatever reason my tornado experience was what was allowing me to see the entities. The most important thing is that I never saw anything that wasn't there, but I saw many things that were there. It would always be difficult to watch the entities around areas of the store as customers got near them. I was constantly expecting something crazy to happen at those times. There would be several times when someone would come in and tell me of seeing something strange outside at night. As I got ready to go out to my car after closing, I saw that the car was filled with spirits. I saw something else that I had not seen previously; there were seven large very shiny discs on different parts of my black car. The discs were each about as large as a tennis ball, and super shiny. As time went on, I realized that the discs would be on a vehicle whenever spirits were sitting in that vehicle. It seemed that each disc represented an entity that was in the vehicle. I never knew the reason why the discs were there, unless it was to let other spirits or believers know that they were in the vehicle. Ever since then, I still find myself routinely observing other cars on dark rainy nights, and you will be surprised how often I see those shiny discs on vehicles in large parking lots. That night I decided to start taking lots of pictures, because I already knew people wouldn't believe most of these things which I was seeing. That decision turned out to be the best evidence to prove to the nonbelievers that ghosts are real, and it made me understand that most people want to avoid the spirit existence. That is a sad fact because we will all, good and bad, be in that form when we die. I got into the habit of always saying to the entities; Sheba and I want to know who is riding with us, so we want to take your picture. That would be my very first interaction with spirits and it would be the beginning of some of the most awesome experiences of my life. As I told the seven men that night, some slightly smiled, others I saw no reaction and only one shook his head okay. Sometimes there would be some who would stare blankly right through you, because I learned that they were in another dimension. I took several pictures that night with my cell phone, and we got into the car. This was the first of tens of thousands of miles riding with spirits that would happen throughout the next 2+ years. That first night I let Sheba jump into the front bucket seat instead of the back seat. The back seat was full already and one was in the front seat. She jumped across my seat into the front passenger seat and instantly started licking the face of an entity that was there already. Then they all wanted to pet her at the same time, and she was enjoying it. It was strange as I was going into the store that I was looking back at my car, filled with the entities surrounding my dog. Next, were my concerns of someone seeing the entities in my car and stopping me to let me know, and what would I say? Fortunately, that only happened one time, in 2012 two local men who were obviously Native American, came up behind my truck in Grove, Oklahoma blowing their horn. I could see what they were motioning to me, so as they turned off behind me, I waved thanks to them. I could for the first time, smell aftershave, cigarette smoke, and beer in my car that night. There were occasions after that when I would detect the odor of beer, whiskey, pot smoke and cigarette smoke, and all at the same time around entities. I also saw cigarette packs and matches in shirt pockets of some of the males, and the cigarettes and matches were popular brands. Sometimes the matches would have the name of a local convenience store.

+ + + + +

I had thousands of questions in my head, with no one who could answer them for me. We got back from the store and went inside my building. Some of the entities stayed in the car while others came into the store with us. As Sheba and I went into our back bedroom, I thought how crazy this all seemed that was happening to me, but that was only beginning. Then I heard radio music which appeared to be coming from out of the attic, and soon another station could be heard in a different location in the building. One was playing some type of rock music and the other had a classical tune playing. If you walked around in the building it was coming from different places. I even went up onto the ladder going into the attic that night, and there it sounded as if it was downstairs. We sat up for a good while after that. After we finally went to bed, I stupidly locked my bedroom door for the first time ever. There were no more problems, which we heard about that night. In the morning, Sunday June 12, it was quiet when we woke up at the usual 7AM. I worked a long tiring day until midnight, and before we walked out the front door, I noticed both of my cars in the parking lot were filled with riders. I locked both outside doors and opened the car door to take the usual pictures. This would turn out to be one of the strangest things I had seen yet. There were six male entities in the car, and right off the bat I noticed there was a real attitude problem. One of them was sitting in the passenger front seat where my dog usually sat. Sheba got along well with most everyone usually, but she had an ability to detect something evil. That would turn out to be an ability that would alert me quickly to potential trouble, and I learned some of it from her. That night she refused to get in the seat with that one entity who was sitting in it, so in a half joking manner; I told him that Sheba didn't want to share her seat for some reason. He just sat there and stared at me like who really cares. I then told him several more times that I wanted him to move, and he refused. Now, that was the first time that I had encountered something like that from them, but that was going to change soon. There truly wasn't much that I could do about it, so I made her go ahead and jump into that seat anyway. I don't know what he was doing to her but she was getting over on the center console to get away from him. Since she weighed about 90 pounds at the time, it was hard balancing her on the console as she was also leaning against me. That night was the first time that I had felt uncomfortable with any of them in my car. Three years later, I would discover that individual colors of their outfits meant something biblically, and that each color represented the level of sin that each was involved in. The level didn't necessarily mean that they I wouldn't be forgiven one day by God, but would have given me a heads up of what I may expect from each of them when in my presence. At that time I would also learn that they were all just regular people in their flesh bodies at one time, but each one still had some level of sin. That would explain that they were exactly like we are today in our flesh bodies, that some of us are good and some are not so good, but we are all sinners. As I drove along I 44 that night, I detected that there was a definite evil undertone within my car. I drove the 30 miles to Joplin and got off on Highway 43 South, where there were three different truck terminals right at the interchange. Since I needed to get fuel, I pulled into the second terminal on the right, and I pulled up to the row of gas pumps directly in front of the store. As I was filling my gas tank, I was watching the interaction of the entities with my dog. It was to become something that I had to be always very aware of, because Sheba was a big part of my life. There would be so many times ahead when I would have to leave her alone in that environment and I never enjoyed it. I would learn how to control those bad situations, and it would soon become necessary for me to do. After I ran my credit card, I went inside the store to get a cup coffee and I noticed there were a lot of people in the store. While I was waiting at the counter to pay for my coffee, I saw a several people pointing to something in the parking lot. I could see that it was a very bright and intense beam of light shining through the front glass doors. The two employees working at the counter were asking each other where the light was coming from. As I left the counter and got closer toward the door, I could plainly see that the light was coming out of my black car right in front. Then one of the employees came out from behind the counter, and he yelled; whose car is that anyway? I thought quickly and told them it was my car, but I couldn't explain where the light was coming from. I had no idea of what I really should do, so I paid for the coffee and briskly walked to my car. It would have gotten even crazier if some of the people had been able to see the ghosts. I had already decided not to tell them who was really shining that bright light, because that would have really caused turmoil. Just as I neared the car, the light went off and I could only determine that it was coming from the back seat. I didn't know anyone in the store that night, but they were sure looking hard at me as I drove off. I would have hundreds of similarly baffling episodes sometimes in much more complex settings. That light was my first experience with spiritual entities being able to bridle electrical current but it would surely not be the last. I would find out that the spiritual entities were able to manipulate electrical energy for just about any purpose, from almost any electrical source. Most importantly, I would begin to understand that the entities have to recharge their spiritual bodies every 24 hours, as if their body is like a battery. Normally they recharge late at night, by exposing themselves to an almost unlimited number of energy sources such as insulated electrical wiring. It would also become knowledge to me that the evil ones would even try to attach themselves to live human bodies to recharge. Learning as much as possible during the months of June and July 2011, I would be able to understand better how to deal with the extra-terrestrial entities that would begin appearing in August. That night as I left the Petro station and drove the remaining 28 miles to my home in Oklahoma, I was in deep contemplation. I had no idea where things were going with this, but I would promise God every night that I wouldn't quit until He said it was time. I had no idea that I was only in basic training, for the real battle that was coming.

As I drove up to my farm gate and turned into my driveway, I realize dome of the entities were already outside the car. I always teasingly told them to make sure to be back by three tomorrow, if they wanted to ride back to the store. The next morning, I looked out my kitchen window, and they all appeared to be back in the car early. I remember asking my wife to look in the car; she looked and obviously could not see the entities. That was what I expected, because most people can't see them except for camera images or mirror images. I stood there beside the car with her that morning, and described what they each were wearing. She told me I was nuts because there was absolutely nothing in that car. I could accept the fact that most people can't see spirits, but the really annoying thing was that she they would not accept that others were able to see them. I would sometimes even take pictures of the entities, and she would instantly say I can't see it. Pictures are clear evidence that anyone can see, but like all photos some are better than others in clarity. I would meet in a short while entities who could choose whether to be revealed in a picture or not. They would be very evil entities from other worlds, that were being brought here secretly by our government for sinister purposes.

The afternoon of Monday June 13 I got to work at 4:30, and a deputy sheriff who patrolled my area at night came by to visit with me. He wanted to introduce a new deputy to me, who was going to begin patrolling that area. We were talking about the tornado from three weeks ago, and he asked me if I had heard about the ghosts at the truck terminal at 71 South Exit. I ask him what was happening there, and both deputies began telling me that the night after the tornado, that kitchen employees had refused to come to work. One of the deputies had driven through the terminal lot at night, and had seen spirits himself and knew that they were real. Supposedly the workers came into work and began seeing spirits in the kitchen area at night. They told me that several of the employees were fired for refusing to come to work after that. A month after this conversation with the deputies, I ran into a former employee of mine, who had been employed with that same terminal business for several years. She had transferred to another company shortly after the tornado, since the company had changed ownership. Apparently, the spirits in the kitchen incident had brought about a sale of that business very shortly after the tornado. New management was put in place and my former employee chose to move to another company. She told me that even her four-year old was able to see the spirits one night right outside the kitchen area. Apparently, the owners of Flying J were Mormons from Salt Lake City Utah, and they falsely believed that the appearance of spiritual entities in their business was the work of Satan. The owners quickly sold the business for that reason.

I then told the two deputies about how the entities had appeared in my building four days after the tornado. I also told them about my experience driving into the edge of the tornado at the Highway 71 South Exit. It was all very interesting to me, that there was absolute proof now that what I was seeing was also seen by others, in another location as well. They were both pretty amazed listening to the story; of all the interactions I had been having with the entities. Yet those two Jasper County Deputies left that afternoon knowing that I was being truthful with them, after all they had told me the original story of the spirits at the 71 South

Exit. It was quite encouraging to me every time I encountered other people, who wholeheartedly acknowledged that the spirits were real. I thanked them both for coming by that afternoon; it was the perfect confirmation that I needed to give others who wanted to disbelieve me. Strangely enough it only seemed to be my wife that didn't believe in spirits. I had been married to her for forty years and had never known it. There had to be some other reason that my wife did not want to believe me, and it would become obvious later.

That night soon after it got dark; I began seeing what appeared to be men, women and children in my building. There was even a small black fuzzy dog with two of the people and even the little dog was playing with Sheba. There appeared to be maybe twenty-five people total and all of them, including the little dog were very friendly and in a quite happy mood. After that evening there were several instances where the people and the same little dog would ride in my cars with me. That night I was sitting in a large red straight-backed chair behind the counter and Sheba was right beside me. Once the entities realized that I accepted them and was not uncomfortable with them, they really started to appear more often. I told him that Sheba was friendly and loved playing with them, and they all got down on Sheba's level and began hugging her. As Sheba began licking their faces, I told them that she would remember every one of them when she saw them again. They really seemed to enjoy hearing that, I believe it meant that I wasn't afraid of them, and that I totally accepted them. I drove home that night after closing, and I had a truck full of friendly passengers. It was a very relaxing ride that evening, and I had a chance to look at all of them real closely. I had an idea that I who I was seeing, were some of the Joplin tornado victims. I had saved a Joplin newspaper from shortly after the tornado, and it had pictures of all the known victims. So the next day, I carried that newspaper back to work with me. That night of June 14, when I got time, I began comparing pictures to my guests. What I began seeing was amazing and so beautiful, and I would be able to match some pictures with the guests.

A few nights later Friday, June 17, around 10 PM, I was standing at my front door facing I- 44, as I did many times during slow evenings. What I began seeing over my building, was yet another one of the most unbelievable sights ever. In the air between the top of my building, and the interstate were as many as 12 ghosts like images that appeared as white kites. They were gliding up and down, rolling over, and generally having a ball. I immediately knew that it was some of my guests, even though this was something which I had never seen. There were three images staying together in flight, two of the images were smaller than the one. I said to myself, I wonder who that is. No sooner than I had said that instantly covered again, and they flew out over the interstate and back. I watched all those different individuals for probably 30-45 minutes, and it was a sight that I will never forget. I never saw that happen again, but I felt there had to be a reason that I was allowed to witness that beautiful event. Seeing them and knowing that they were real and alive, was a most special gift from God.

I had been staying overnight more at the store, and we would go home during the day, several times a week. So many different things were happening that I needed to be there more. Also, C was getting her hours mostly on days during the week, rather than weekends. I would stay over the weekend, and work most every night during the week as well. By Friday June 24, my employee knew what was going on, but the entities did not come around her very often. I discovered that the friendly spirits never want to be around anyone who is uncomfortable with them. I knew that the evil ones didn't care whether you wanted them around or not, and they are the ones that you don't want around you. On Friday evening June 24, I stayed over several days and nights without going home. So, I decided with C to open the next morning. We drove home that evening after closing at midnight; as usual we had riders, but no problems that night.

Saturday June 25, was a beautiful and clear summer day. I had made plans with C that I would relieve her by 3:30 PM, since she had made plans with her children for late afternoon. I left my home around 2:15, expecting that I would have enough time to get there. I was driving my late model Dodge Quad Cab pickup that afternoon, which still had the original factory tires on it. My business was located at exit 26, the Sarcoxie exit on I -44, east of Joplin. My usual route was Missouri Highway 43 N. to I-44 interchange at Joplin, then I-44 E. to exit 26. This was seemingly just another Saturday afternoon drive to work. I was about 5 miles from my home, when I felt my right rear tire hit something in the edge of the road. I never knew what it was that I hit, but it had cut a large puncture in the sidewall of the rear tire. As I approached Roark Creek, my tire blew out, so I turned left beside the creek, and pulled off the road next to the woods. Since I had changed many tires in my lifetime, I only saw this as an untimely and sweaty inconvenience. Since I was parked on a flat glassy area with no traffic nearby, I assumed it would only take a few minutes to change the tire. The truck had large all-terrain tires on it and there was a new spare in the rack underneath. Since I had never accessed that tire, I could not determine how to get the tire out of the rack. Someone had broken into my truck months earlier and took the service manual out of the glove box. I spent 15 to 20 minutes trying to make a call with my cell phone, but I had no phone signal. I went to a house nearby and there was no one was at home. I knew now that I was going to be late in relieving my employee, and it was going to interfere with her plans with her children. I walked the 50 yards out to the highway to flag someone down. I waved at people as they drove by to get someone to stop. This went on for at least 45 minutes without anyone stopping. It seemed the few people who came along, were out for an afternoon drive and thought I was just being friendly. Finally, I saw a white Chevrolet pickup coming around the curve, and first thing that I noticed about the truck was that it had a tire changing rack in the back, the next thing I saw was that they were stopping. The truck immediately turned left onto the grassy area close to where my truck was. A tall older very white-haired gentleman was driving, and another man who was probably in his 50s was also in the truck. The first thing the older gentleman said was "what's the matter son." First thing I said to him jokingly was; God must have sent you. That statement from me was an old southern expression which I had heard used all my life. Coming from me it wasn't meant to have any religious connotation, because I had very little religious ties at that time. The old gentleman looked intently at me and replied, **"maybe He did."** When he answered that way, I felt my hair instantly standing up on the back of my neck. I had no idea why that happening at the time, except that his was words seem so true. I explained to them what my problem was in not being able to change my tire. He said that's no problem we can handle that for you, and he told his son to pull their truck around closer to my truck. He told me that his son would change it for me, but that he had to have my jack handle in order to release the tire from the rack. I again told him that I would change the tire if I could only find out to get the spare down, instead he said no lets you and I sit down and visit some. He said my son will get that tire changed for you while we get to know each other. I was 65 at the time, and it appeared that his son was probably in his early 50s. I decided that the older gentleman was probably near 80 years old, and I had a strong feeling that something about this man was special. At that time, I still had little if any comprehension of how all these things happening in my life were connecting. My life was certainly not in any Christian mode at that point in my life, just because things very strange had happened to me during the tornado and since. I was hearing all the disbelief from my wife concerning everything that was happening to me, and I was not really happy that day. Little did I know that afternoon, but God had a plan in motion that was going propel me deep into a world that would become spiritually awesome. With such unknowing prophetic fashion my wife was going to tell me; "you just want to be like someone in the Bible." Little did I understand how she was the person, who was going to help create the Biblical likeness of the story? I would only be a witness who would become the storyteller.

The son was now changing the tire and his father, and I continued our conversation. The old gentleman looked at me and said" Well what's going on in your life, son?" Once again, I had that prickly sensation along the back of my neck. I instantly had a strong feeling that this man must be a religious person, and that I had to tell him literally everything. I also just felt a dread that he was going to ask me what kind of business I had. I had told him that I was on the way to my business to relieve an employee. Then I told him my life was fine except that I had a situation with some spirits at my business. He looked at me quizzically and asked, "what kind of spirits son"? I told him that they were mostly friendly and were men, women and children. He seemed totally engrossed in the details of the story as it unfolded. He reached over and put his arm on my shoulder, and he asked me how close the Joplin Tornado had been to my business. I felt that this man was about to explain things to me that I didn't understand at all. I began telling him about May 22, and how Sheba and I had driven into the tornado that Sunday afternoon. He looked intently at me, with his arm still on my shoulder, and he said" Son, those poor souls are just searching for the way home and they will leave before long." He went on to explain to me, that I had probably been allowed by God, to enter briefly into the world of the spiritual afterlife for some reason. He then added that those spirits had encountered me at that site of the tornado and had just followed me back. The kindly old gentleman then told me that he had been a minister for many years in a Pentecostal Church, and that he had been around many spiritual entities in his life. Since I had detected something special about him all the time that was it, and he was like a breath of fresh air explaining things to me that did make sense after all. I then told him about all the close interactions that I was having with the spirits, and how strange it all felt. The quiet spoken old minister then added something that I was already learning about the good spirits. It was a rule that the good spirits will not stay around you, unless you are comfortable in their being there. He said God is likely allowing them to be around you so much, for a "bigger purpose and only God knows what that is." He also so correctly told me that there was probably another day coming, when God would introduce me to the world of evil spirits as well. Additionally, he told me that my being able to see the spirits was a gift, and that he had also had that ability most of his life as well. Then the knowing old pastor intrigued me, when he told me that my being able to interact so freely with the spirits was something that he had never heard of. He then added, but you eventually will learn to look at them, and know quickly whether they are good or bad. He was to be correct in that statement just like all the other advice he had given me.

As we were finishing up our informative conversation, his son had finished changing my tire and had even put the flat tire into my truck. We got up off the grass where we had been sitting and I shook hands with both of the men. I asked them how much I owed them for the tire fix. They were both shaking their heads that nothing was owed. I insisted that I pay them for the work, and I even tried to put two $20 dollar bills in their hands. They told me they were just happy that they had decided to drive that way that day. The old gentleman then told me; "we never drive this way from Anderson to our farm because it is way out of the way, but today something told me to come this way." I had that same feeling once again as he said that and the hairs on my neck stood up. I thanked them again for their help; and they waved back with big smiles on their faces, as they drove away. As I was driving on to my store, I realized that without a doubt that I had just encountered two very special people in a most unusual manner. However, the most extraordinarily beautiful experience ever in my life was to appear in slightly more than an hour. That event would be the foundation from which much more understanding would come forth. Over the next couple of years, several times I would think about trying to look the men up just to update them on my life. Yet regretfully, I never went further in trying to locate them. Then in the summer of 2013 ironically, I met a couple while I was changing a tire on my car who had known the old gentleman. They told me that they thought that he passed away sometime in late 2011 and that he was probably in his early 80s. I always felt so bad that I never was able to tell him how much he had spiritually taught me that hot June afternoon. He was a big player in explaining that probably God had a hand in the appearance of the spirits in my life. The kindly old pastor was the very first to recognize that the "poor souls" were from the tornado, and that" they had just followed me back." He also told me they were just looking for the way home, and that they would eventually find their way out. Like so many people who would become involved in God's Plan for me, I will never forget that wonderful old man and his son. They were a beautiful part of carrying out the plan in helping to get me to that store right before the *angel* would appear precisely at 5pm. Without their showing up at that time, I would have been a long time getting the tire changed, and would likely have been much later getting to the store. When I had said God must have sent you, his answer was the correct one when he said" maybe he did." I didn't know then that it was evidence of the Holy Spirit's Presence, when I had felt my hair prickling up on my neck at several things he said.

The time was 3:45 when I left Roark Creek that afternoon, and it still was a good hour to the store. I wasn't able to call my employee at the store until I got almost to Joplin. I informed her that I had had a tire problem, and I would be there in about half an hour. When I walked into the store it was exactly 4:50 PM, and she had one customer in the store. I told C I would let her have the whole day off Sunday because of my being so late getting in. She clocked out at 4:55, and the one customer left right behind her. I had planned to stay over that night and work both shifts Sunday until closing. My loyal Rottweiler Sheba, who was always close to me, had followed me into the back office as the last customer drove away.

Precisely at 5 PM, I saw a Medium Blue Buick pulling into my front parking area. The brand-new car had parked in the one parking space, which was directly in line with my glass front door. The automobile still had a new car dealer's license plate from Branson, Missouri on the front. I got up and walked back up to the front counter where I usually tried to greet incoming customers. Sheba came and stood right beside as I was standing at the counter. I observed a well-dressed, quite attractive, maybe early fifties lady get out and walk in through the front door. As owner of the business for years, I was accustomed to seeing workers, doctors, lawyers, truck drivers, housewives, and all in between as customers. Yet, this uniquely attractive woman didn't seem to fit anywhere within my any of my usual customer profiles. After a lot of years in retail sales, you learn a lot about customers just by observing them as they walk in. Something about this customer seemed much different than anyone I had ever seen come through that door. The attractive woman with the perfect coiffure was there standing directly in front of us across the counter. At that point, Sheba did something that she rarely ever did; she jumped up and put both her front feet on the counter, which allowed her to make eye contact with a visitor. Then the smiling visitor turned her head a bit and said charmingly *"I'll bet I have driven by this little building 1000 times and I never ever saw it"*. The store really was difficult to see from the highway, because it was constructed on a much lower level than the interstate. She incredibly had one of the most pleasant voices that I had ever recalled hearing, and her ice-breaking statement ended with such a beautiful smile. Then she went on to tell me that she lived in Branson, and that she was involved in filming a documentary concerning the Joplin tornado damages. She added that she had made a lot of trips back and forth to Joplin since the tornado. She told me a good bit of personal information about herself and about her late husband. She told me that she had been raised in Springfield and only recently had come back to the area to live. She then looked at me teasingly and said; **"you're probably too young to remember me," but I was a singer with the Billy Graham Crusades for many years."** She was kiddingly complimentary about me being too young to remember, because she was obviously a bit younger than I. She said she and her husband had lived in another large city in the south, and that after Dr. Billy Graham became ill health she had decided to retire. She also told me that her husband was killed during the cleanup of the New Orleans Hurricane Katrina, so she had bought her old home place in Springfield, Missouri which had been her mothers, but that she was now actually residing in Branson. She then told me that she was returning from Joplin that afternoon and as she passed the exit 26 ramp, she noticed a troubled looking young man standing beside the road. She said that he was standing in front of his car with the hood raised up, and he had his shirt off and looked so forlorn that she felt sorry for him. She then began reciting a most amazingly beautiful narrative of her conversation with God in a most calm quiet voice; I said **"God should I help that young man; he looks so troubled? And God said, No, I have something more important for you to do right now."** Then she said," **God where should I go?"** and **God said;" go up to the next intersection and turn around and come back."** Then she said, **"God should I turn around at the KuminGo?" and He said yes."** Then she said **"so I went up to the KuminGo intersection and started back this way, "and I said where I should I go now God? "And God said, you will recognize it "so as I passed your store, I asked God is that it?**

God said, "yes that's it." Then I said; "God how do I get to it? And God said, go down to the next intersection and come back up the side road."

Then as she was still standing directly across the counter facing me, with that beautiful, pleasant smile on her face, she asked; **"So is that you?"** I was only thinking: **Is that me what?** Although somehow, I did know that it was me, yet I had no idea who she was or what she wanted with me. I then did something that was so out of character; I started to cry, and the crying then became so uncontrollable that I couldn't even speak. Then with Sheba right beside me, I felt as if by some power I was being drawn around that counter. I felt an indescribable urge to stand face to face with that most Holy Spirit filled person that I had ever heard of. I walked around the counter to where she was standing, and I stood directly in front of her within 18 inches of her face. She was standing in front of a mirrored display rack which faced the counter, and I was standing with my back to the counter. I remember that Sheba sat down beside me on my right side. With my knowing how always attentive Sheba was to my emotions, I feel certain that she was watching and listening intently to everything that was going on. Sheba's' number one priority always was protecting me from harm. She also had a most unique ability for knowing when something was bothering me, and those times she would come and try to lick my hand or face, depending how serious it seemed to her. If she could have reached my face, she would have been trying to lick away my tears. Sheba had never seen me cry before that day, so I am certain that she was quite concerned. I was still crying so much that I couldn't speak, so I stood serenely in front of this most obvious Messenger from God. That entire incident happened before I learned that certain pictures would not be allowed to be recorded on my surveillance camera log. I suppose I looked a hundred times for that event on my surveillance recordings, but was never even able to find the frame of her car driving up. She then reached out with both of her hands, and took hold of my left hand and arm. I said to her;" Why am I crying so much, I never ever cry about anything?" and I told her that I never even cried at funerals. She replied in that beautiful kind voice" **It's the Holy Spirit honey, it's okay; God doesn't want us to be hard like that; and you will never again be that way.**" As I was slowly trying to wipe away the tears, she was steadily squeezing my left arm and hand and smiling softly, yet with a most serious demeanor.

She then looked more intently into my eyes, and in that soft, kind voice she said this;" **God is about to bestow a very special gift upon you.**" *I thought instantly, why in the world would God want to give me of all people, a special gift?*

She knew everything that I was feeling before I could even say it. She answered that first thought by saying, **"God doesn't see the bad in us; he only sees the good."** Then she answered the next thought I had. **"This is not about your adult business; it is much more important than that. God needs you for an ability that you have, something that He wants you** to **do for him."** Then she said this; **"I don't know how bad it will be or how long it will last, because He never tells me those things."** and she added; **"but God will never forsake you, and He will always do more than you ask of Him. "**While now still holding both my hands, she asked me if I would permit her to ask one question of me as she recorded my answer. I told her that I would, and she told me that she needed to get her recorder out of the car. I was still in shock as she walked out to her car and came back with a small audio recorder. That surprised me, because I assumed she was going to video record my answer. Her one question was **"where is the coldest place in your entire building?"** I found that question so strange, because I had mentioned nothing about ghosts in my building to her. I responded to her that the coldest spot was in my far back storage room. I never fully understood for a long time why she wanted to ask that on the voice recorder. However, many months later I would clearly understand her reason for that recorded question. God had obviously made known to her that evil entities were eventually going to enter my journey. I am certain that that beautiful *angel* has prayed for me many times, over the last several years since that Saturday June 25 in 2011. One day I do believe that I will meet that "beautiful angel" again, and we will talk about that most memorable June afternoon.

✦✦✦✦✦✦

I do believe that God wanted my answer to that question recorded for some reason, and that was fine with me. She smiled, hugged my neck, and walked toward the door. She stopped and turned around at the door and in that same beautiful voice, she repeated what she had said earlier; **"Remember no matter how bad it gets, God will never forsake you."** There was no doubt from what she said; she did know that "It" would really get bad probably for a long time. However, she would be proven 100% correct about; God never forsaking me and doing more than I ever ask of him. The *angel* then walked out the door, got in her car and drove away. Sheba and I stood at the door for several long minutes after she left, trying to sort through all of the overwhelming emotions that I was feeling. I knew that God was really taking over my life for some purpose. I felt empowered by it, but I did not have one person yet, who I could share my overwhelming emotions with. The encounter earlier that afternoon, with the old pastor had not been an accident either. It was another confirming piece of evidence of God's Intervention in my life. Now in addition to everything else that had transpired, a real live Angel of God had appeared to me, *of all people*, with news of *a very special Gift from God*. I knew that it was real, but I also knew that I would have countless times to analyze it all. It seemed that I was allowed those few minutes after the "angel" left, just so that I could fully appreciate that feeling. For in the instant that I walked back behind the counter, several cars were coming into the parking lot. Every single time a spiritual event like this would happen in the future, business would end until the event was over. Only God could make those kinds of things happen, and I understood that without a doubt. Those same patterns would become a familiar routine in the weeks and months ahead.

It was now slightly past 5:30 PM, and the *"angel"* had stayed there exactly 30 minutes. I would understand almost two years later that her arrival at precisely 5PM on June 25th had meant something special. Biblically Number 5 means the Grace of God and Number 25 means the Double Grace of God. Both Biblical numerical meanings had been bestowed upon me that afternoon and they would both represent me being saved.

Then it hit me like a ton of bricks: the memory of another hot Saturday June 25th, almost 30 years earlier, when I had also been bestowed with the Double Grace of God. Without being location specific, that hot June afternoon my partner and I were on a mission in a foreign country that was unfriendly to the United States. We had just been surprised by a large enemy patrol boat with 25-30 men appearing on deck with automatic weapons locked and loaded. There were also several .50 cal. deck-mounted cannons that were trained on us, just as we were about to enter the mouth of the river. It was immediately obvious that we were heavily outnumbered and way outgunned, and only 50 meters apart. My partner and I had been together in some tough places over the years, and we had an abundance of confidence in ourselves. However, it felt like we may have finally run out of luck, and it just might be the end of the trail. We quickly exchanged hugs and a few words and agreed that life had been a good ride. I am now ashamed to recall that I certainly didn't call on God and I seriously doubt that my partner did either. Neither of us had much of a Godly relationship, yet that day without either one of us calling on Him, God delivered us a miracle from a most unlikely ally. Without a doubt only God could have enabled us to pull off the maneuver which allowed us to avoid a certain fate. We were going to either die then or be locked away in Fidel Castro's underground prison forever, and those were the options had God not intervened. So, I now know for a fact that God bestowed a special gift upon me and my partner that Saturday afternoon June 25, and that first Double Grace Intervention saved my flesh body. Now many years later, ironically on the same exact day and date, God would again intervene in my life but this time He would save my body and my soul. They were both in the same bad shape as they were that day many years earlier in another country. This Saturday June 25, 2011 God had again intervened in my life and in a much more dramatic manner. With all my sins, He still had that same plan for me that I was going to participate in, and this time He had also saved me from the certain consuming fires of Hell. Months later, when things would really get tough and I had learned to call on him He would always tell me;" don't worry about the one who can kill your flesh body, but worry about the one who can cause your soul and spirit to perish." Now that it had been four weeks since the tornado, everything that was happening was beginning to make some sense, but little did I know how much bigger things were going to get. While I knew, that I wasn't anything close to what God expected of a Christian, it seemed that He was temporarily accepting me even as as I was. That was what was so baffling to me that God had chosen me of all people, but I was still pretty much the same person. As it turned out, I was beginning to change slowly but my survival would be a priority for a while yet. It would still be a long time before I would really start to fully accept all the beautiful happenings. I knew that wife was never going to believe this latest event either, or I was certain of that. I would realize after May 22, 2011, and both the June 25ths, that God had seen fit to provide such an amazing testimony in my life.

My wife and I had enjoyed a good marriage of 40+ years, as of June 2010. I would learn that the number 40 in Biblical Meaning is Trials and Probation. We surely had survived the probationary period I would have thought, but the real trials were about to begin. During the last 4 years, since her mother's death in 2007, our marriage had been coming unwound. Earlier in our marriage, I had had several brief affairs with other women. My wife had still remained very loyal to me through all those times. We had raised three beautiful children, two girls and one boy, and she had always made sure they were in church on Sundays. I can remember so many times that I did not go to church with them yet I could have, because I was at home. I can also remember times, when I was literally out of the country, my wife usually not knowing where I was, or if I would make it back safely. I was always thankful during those days, for having such a caring, loving wife who always took good care of the children. Even though my relationship with God was barely existent, I would frequently say to myself and a few others, of how thankful I was to God for my wife. I know that I may not have considered God in most of my life, but God had definitely not forgotten about me. I had always provided well for my family, and I loved them dearly. By the time we had moved from southern Oklahoma to the Grand Lake area in 2006, it had been many years since my last affair with another woman. Once we had to leave southern Oklahoma, to be nearer to the Missouri business, my wife had to leave a very good position with a hospital. I know that was part of her unhappiness with moving and was understandable. My mother-in-law died in early 2007, and the marriage seemed to have really started deteriorating after her death. That is not to say that it was entirely my wife's fault, because we were both relating to each other poorly. My mother-in-law and I had many disagreements over the years, but for the last 10 years or so her life we had gotten our differences resolved. She was a very independent, beautiful person, in excellent health right up past her 93rd birthday. She lived with us the last eight months of her life, and she much regretted the feeling, that she had lost her independence. I know that my wife began to suffer emotionally from watching her mother's health deteriorate towards the end of her life. My mother in law had had always been seen as a strong individual, who never wanted to even discuss sickness or death. As young children, my wife and her two siblings were hardly allowed to ever be sick and miss school. I know that she suffered, watching the deterioration of her mother's health. I saw her mother's death becoming eminent, and I encouraged my wife to resolve any past disagreements in their lives. I believe that there were some unresolved regrets between them, but those things were not our only problems in the marriage. Things from both our past and current lives were creating a Perfect Storm for the Devil

After moving to northeast Oklahoma, I still had to manage a good-sized residential land development in southern Oklahoma, as well as a failing power-sports business that we had in Montgomery, Alabama. The project in southern Oklahoma was 340 miles each way to drive, for me continue marketing the home sites. The Alabama business was 735 miles each way, but I finally decided to close it down in 2009, due to the failing economy. We were trying to sell the Missouri business, but the economy had prohibited buyers from getting financing and I didn't want to hold the financing personally. I'll admit, I too was stressed from the logistics of everything. I definitely was not easy to get along with in those days, and that contributed in the marriage problems as well.

I decided to add some new things into the Missouri business inventory. My plan was to offer more incentives that would attract more prospective buyers for the store. In early 2010, we decided to expand our lingerie marketing in the store, by adding much more selection. We were already carrying several different top brands, and we added a name brand Italian lingerie inventory. We bought in quantities, which gave us the ability to sell at slightly above wholesale to the public. We were selling the exact lingerie as the top lingerie retailer in the country, and we were selling at 25-30 % less than they were. We were truly selling top lingerie almost full wholesale, and doing well at it. We also decided to hire attractive lingerie models to model our inventory inside the store. The models were able to earn very good money part time or full time. This was a quite successful move, except it added to the perfect storm that was already swirling in our marriage. I kept several models on the shifts six days a week, they were off on Sundays. I hired some part-time college students from surrounding areas, as well as several full time models. I tried to hire models that fit the "attractive girl next door look" and had hired several different models beginning in July 2010, and then I hired a new girl during the last week of July. That girl, who I will call A, really worked out well. She sold lots of lingerie, as well as modeling before and after sales. She was very personable and very attractive and she created lots of sales for the store. She also had a charisma that few managers ever appreciate, but buyers are much more attracted to persons with that charisma. Without really knowing it, this manager was attracted to her beauty and charisma, and it would lead to me becoming involved with her for nearly three months. None of the modeling was nude or even semi-nude, but it was all totally tasteful modeling of classy lingerie. A, in early September, asked if she could rent a house from me that was on my property behind the business. I agreed to rent it to her, since she had lost her car, and couldn't get to work. She moved in and started working lots of early mornings, and I went home every night then. Then, without me planning it she and I became involved in a three-month affair. I believe that affair even though it was wrong, would be a bond that would help save my life more than a year later. That affair right or wrong was related to my unraveled relationship with my wife. Nevertheless with two people now working days, it gave me more time to handle other things since either A or C, was able to manage the counter alone. Whenever I was in the store A would then work as a lingerie model. A stayed until December 10, 2010 and she went back to her ex husband in another state. I had asked A to leave early December, even though she had been a very good employee. After she left people constantly asked what had happened to her, and maybe I should have not forced her to leave when I did. Even though things were just getting to be too much to deal with, I was still sorry to see her go. I really never expected to see her again but she would return at a time in January 2012, and would be a first hand witness to the most unbelievable experiences of my life. Her being present at that time also would help confirm some of the events that would happen while she was there. A would stay with me that time for more than three months, and those three months would be during a period when the enemy was actively trying to take me out. I believe that A helped save my life by being there during that time period.

The night of June 25, 2011, was quiet after the late afternoon revelation from the *angel*. That night near closing time, both of my cars in the parking lot had six or more entities in each car. As I locked up that night, the visitors were all still sitting in the cars.

All images were automatically saved on the main computer for 90 days. I had also been taking many pictures with my cell phone. I couldn't stop thinking about the visit from the angel as I began referring to her. It was so strange listening to her describing her conversation with God, and to think it was all about me, of all people. I found it so difficult, yet so intriguing, to imagine a relationship with God like she obviously had. Listening to her relating the conversation about me with God was so awesome. I had never encountered anything like that in my life. I wasn't even sure that I knew anyone else who had either.

I had a hard time going to sleep that night, because my mind was processing a million things. I slept later on Sunday morning than usual. I went to Sarcoxie, bought breakfast and brought it back to the store. I always bought enough, that I could share it with Sheba, even though she had dog feed available all the time. She really enjoyed eating part of whatever I had at any meal. I stayed all day Sunday, closed at 10:30 Sunday evening, and drove home. I would always think about telling my wife the latest when I got home, but it was beginning to be so painful. I had no one to tell this awesomely beautiful story to except my wife. Instead, when I got home after 1:30 AM, I took a shower went to sleep. I woke up the next morning early, it was Monday, June 27, 2011, and was our 41st wedding anniversary. I was going in later that day and work until 6:30 PM, and then I planned to meet my wife at the Red Lobster in Joplin for dinner. I decided to tell her that morning, about the visit that I had from the "angel", a day and a half ago. It was like 7:30 that morning, and since wasn't going to open until 9:30; it gave me an hour before leaving for work.

I was pouring myself a cup of coffee in the kitchen, when my wife came in. I told her I wanted to tell her about something that had happened over the weekend. She already knew about the flat tire Saturday, but not about the *angel* visiting. I had decided to wait and tell her that in person. I poured myself a cup of coffee, and sat down in the living room. I began telling her about what had happened Saturday afternoon at 5 o'clock. I told her that I knew, without a doubt, it was a more beautiful experience than I could have ever imagined. I added to that statement, M it really happened just as I have told you. It is part of everything beautiful that is happening, and I so wish you would believe me.

I then told her then, how the old pastor had also been part of the story, by his explaining things that I didn't understand, about the spirits that I was seeing. She was just staring at me, and saying nothing.

Then when she spoke, this is what she said **"I think you are just trying to be like someone in the Bible."** Of all the strange things she could have said, that statement just floored me. I cannot explain how it made me feel, but I realized that what I was going through was truly beginning to sound like a story of the Bible. However I had no control over anything that was happening. I also knew it was so true and that God was making it all happen. It was the most painful feeling to be accused of hallucinating by the most important person in my life. It was still a beautiful feeling as well, and I could alleviate the pain by knowing that God would not allow his work to be called a lie forever. I would continually assure my wife that I would be vindicated by God one day and I still know that.

✦ ✦ ✦ ✦ ✦

I got up and finished getting ready to leave for work. All day, I could not stop thinking about my wife and our conversation that morning. She had told me for many years, how she always prayed that God would someday change me. Now on our 41st wedding anniversary, I tell her about the most beautiful happening ever in our lives, and she couldn't accept the fact that maybe ironically her prayers had been answered. Now that God was changing me, I had no one to even tell about it. I remembered how the" angel" had told me that God didn't want me to be emotionless, and that I would never be like that again. Now I have emotions about all of this, but none of my immediate family cares to hear about my feelings. I knew that my wife was telling my three children aged 25, 27, and 29, that I was hallucinating. Two of my children lived in Tulsa, and the oldest, a Registered Nurse, lived in Montgomery Alabama. Ironically, she was the Director of a Mental Health facility there. The children all believed their mother, even though I talked to them regularly. What my wife was doing, was to become more bizarre than any story ever told in the Bible. My son came over from Tulsa that afternoon of our anniversary, and I told her to ask him to dinner with us. We met for dinner around seven in Joplin, and I could tell that he was quite uncomfortable discussing any of the things going on. Yet, I knew that he had to be aware of my mental stability just by talking to me. I knew that it had to be confusing and disturbing, to hear the different stories that he was hearing from his mother. It was a quiet, less than enjoyable evening and my wife and son left soon after the meal. I went back to work more confused than ever but feeling about as unhappy as I ever had in my life. I knew that my beautiful home and farm wasn't a pleasant place anymore, while I knew that this should be the happiest time of our life. I kept thinking that maybe my wife just had some sort of problem accepting things that these things were really happening to me. I hoped that she would wake up and know that it was all real, and that we were truly the luckiest family in the world. Yet, somehow in the back of my mind, I thought maybe for some reason, she was intentionally denying what she knew was true. I couldn't imagine why a wife would ever want to deny, even the possibility that such a beautiful experience, was happening to a husband of 40+ years. That truth was going to come out, but higher levels of family drama were to come before the truth would be exposed.

The spiritual significance of each event seemed to go one notch higher with every episode. I just kept wondering how many notches higher it was going, but I had a strong feeling that it was all going much higher.

I had hired a new lingerie model a week earlier and she was to start work on Tuesday, June 28. I had temporarily discontinued the modeling, when the spirits had moved inside the store on June 11. Now I knew that I had to get things back to normal as well as I could. I just didn't realize what "normal" was going to be from then on. The store was losing money by not having the modeling available. So I had made myself a mental note, to resume the modeling before July 1. The new model we will call S, came in to work at 3:30 in the afternoon on Tuesday, June 28. I had made S aware of the spirits that were in the store, when I hired her a week ago. She was all right with it, as far as she knew. She was also good friends with the other girl S, who had given me the cross in late May. The model S began working that afternoon, and we had a good afternoon and evening. Business became really slow around 11 that evening, and I let her off. I stayed over that night, because I had an early morning business appointment in Joplin, on Wednesday the 29th. That night, Sheba and I went to bed shortly after I closed at midnight. Entities in the store had been coming into my bedroom as I slept, and I had not been closing my bedroom door. I had gotten used to them coming into my room and running their fingers through my hair. I told a couple of friends about it, and they had a hard time imagining how I could have gotten used to the hair thing. However, a few nights earlier I had been out in the front parking lot talking on my cell phone. I was standing near my car, and I heard the automatic door locks clicking in my car. As I watched, the entities who I was accustomed to seeing were inside the car as usual. Then I saw several tall males, appearing to be the same ones who were in the colored jumpsuits, all standing next to the car. These were the original ones who had come inside first on June 11. Then, when the spirits who I believed to be of the tornado victims showed up, the original spirits in red, yellow and blue outfits had temporarily disappeared. It appeared that the entities in the colored outfits were not able to just walk through the doors into the cars. Yet the other spirits could walk through anything, it seemed. I never fully understood what the difference was, between the paranormal abilities of each type of entity. That explained, why the males in the colored outfits, had all come in through the open front door on the morning of June 11. After that incident with the door locks, I began closing and locking my bedroom door that night. Since then, I had been awakened by hearing my door lock being turned and tampered with, sometimes several times each night. That had gotten slightly disturbing, never knowing who or what was on the other side of the door. So that particular night after we went to bed, I was barely a sleep, before I heard the doorknob being twisted on, followed by several knocks on the door. I told whoever it was to get away from the door, but that didn't work. I had a small nightlight on the wall above my bed that cast a glow around the door. As I rose out of bed, I saw a white hand and fingers coming slowly under the door, palm side up. I quietly picked up my gun that was in the corner, and I brought the stock of the gun down on the white hand, firmly against the concrete. There was a most unusual shrill scream from behind the door, as the hand was jerked away. There was no further problems at all that night, but yet never truly understood that experience. I had been taught an awful lot about the spirit world for some reason, but that was yet to be learned. I had noticed that the spirits would nearly always appear in regular type clothing during the daytime and evening. The unfriendly entities liked to appear in white ghost form really late at night. The only time that I ever saw the friendly ones in white ghost form, was the one night that they were flying around the building and over the interstate. I believe that the mean intentioned ones felt that the white ghost image was more frightening to anyone they encountered. I learned very quickly, that the evil ones enjoyed doing things that caused dissension between people. They would move your keys around and electronically turn off the alarm clock, or your cell phone alarm. They could make things appear as if someone around you had moved them. Later they would do things much more serious, in order to cause bigger problems.

One night there were two women, who appeared in my car as I started home. I could usually observe from the store cameras, which was in my vehicle, before I went out to leave. I had noticed that there were mostly only males riding in my vehicles at night. That night in late June 2011, as I took my usual picture before getting into the car, I kiddingly commented that there were only men in the car that night. The next night that I looked at the cameras, before going out to my car, there appeared a basket of faded roses in the picture. I wondered what it meant, as I locked up and went out to get in the car. The faded roses had appeared on the front dashboard in the store camera, but when I opened the car door, the faded roses in spirit form, were in the front seat.

There were two women in the car who I felt were from the 40- 50s era. One had shorter black hair and the other had a reddish brown longer hair. From that time on, the roses would always appear in the car, whenever they were in it. One of these women was the one seen with the two little ones flying around the building in white ghost form, on the night of June 17th. After that night with the roses, those two women became frequent passengers in my vehicles. A couple of nights after the episode when the roses first appeared, I drove my truck to the convenience store after closing. I saw the roses in my truck as I got in. I had a habit of talking to Sheba as I drove along, and quite frequently, I would notice some of the riders would be interested in our conversation. That night, I was listening to the radio; all of a sudden I began smelling perfume that was not familiar to me. As I pulled into the convenience store parking lot, it occurred to me that, that perfume was from a long time ago, and that it belonged to those two women. It was such a beautiful thought to know for sure that they were still alive in a spiritual body and that they only wanted to be acknowledged. It was one of those many encounters that made me give much thought to life after death. That perfume dated those attractive women as having lived in the flesh a long time ago, but I also knew that they were alive still today. Before all these encounters, I truly was not sure that there was life after death. I realized that night, that I was really becoming a softer person, just as the "angel" had promised I would. I thought a lot that night, after I got back into my truck and drove back to the business. I was slowly changing, and I had no control over how it was happening, and those changes were preparing me for some bigger challenges. Throughout the rest of 2011, 2012, and much of 2013, I would collect many thousands more awesome pictures as well as experiences and memories. However, of all the encounters and pictures, the Faded Roses were one of my favorites, solid proof that I was becoming a softer person.

As of Friday, July 8, 2011, the new lingerie model S had been working ten days so far. S was making a few lingerie sales, but I really was accustomed to the models working out better than she had so far. Yet, I could see that I would need to hire at least one more model. I still had my other long time employee C, but had cut back her hours due to my being in the store so much. Since my life at home was not very pleasant, I had been staying over several days and nights at the time at the store. The new employee had her automobile in the shop, so I had to start taking her home at night for a few days. Fortunately', it was only about six or 7 miles to where she lived. I still told her that I really couldn't guarantee that too long, if she didn't get her car out of the shop soon. One of the requirements when I hired someone was that they had an automobile. Early on Friday always began the weekend so we were very usually busy Friday evenings. We closed at midnight as usual, and I took S to her home near Sarcoxie. She told me that she had someone who would bring her into work the next day, Saturday, July 9. I stayed over at the business that night without anything unusual, except that which was normal with all the regular guests. Saturday was pretty slow until noon and business began to get steady. Then when S came in at 2 PM, she got really busy and was like busy all afternoon and evening. Many times after it was really busy for several hours, everything would quiet down well before closing. Ironically S had made far more sales than on any other day in the two weeks she had worked. That would be interesting because that would be her last day working for us. It was 11:15 when the last customer left the store. When business slowed that late, I would allow the employee to leave early if they wanted to. Since I had to give her a ride home again, she would have to stay until I closed at midnight. She was sitting at the counter doing nothing, and I went in the back to finish up some paperwork as I always did at closing. I usually constantly glanced at the cameras out of habit, and less frequently after business slowed near closing time.

All of a sudden S screamed that there was a little man at the front door, who "looked like 1960." Those were her exact words, and I will never forget that description of my Dad. I looked at the two cameras over each side of the front door, and there he was. I jumped up and ran out of my office; there on the main monitor was my father who had died in 1964. His clothing was exactly as I remembered from the 1960s, and though it had been 47 years, I even remembered his sweater that he was wearing. I was yelling all those things to her as I told her to follow me. My dad was looking up at the Red Adult Open sign that was lit over my door. S and I ran to the door, and I went one way and she went the other looking for him. I had a 3 acre parking lot along I -44 that was well lit, but there was not one vehicle in the entire parking lot. Neither was there any sign of my dad anywhere. We went back into the building and started to close up, since it was close to midnight. After we locked up the side doors, we sat back down at the counter. I explained to her that my dad had died in January 1964. My dad was only 68 years old when he died, and I was 18 years old. He and my mother were truly Christians, in the strongest sense. We always attended church every Sunday Morning and Evening in the warmer months, and every Sunday Morning in the winter. He didn't just talk about eternal life in Heaven; he lived life in all the ways, which the Bible promised would assure us of eternal life in Heaven. My dad was also a very intelligent person, who seemed to perceive so many things that were yet to come. There were certain things which he had told me would transpire in the world, that have happened and are still happening many years after his death. He and his cousin were planning to go to college together and eventually attend law school. Right before actually committing to college, my dad decided that his mother needed him to stay and help manage their farm. His cousin went on to college and became a successful attorney and judge, while my dad stayed on that farm his entire life. He and his brother were successful farmers together for many years. He and my mother loved and honored God and taught us well, as we were growing up. It was just that I had little interest in Biblical Teachings and I went off in other directions but God didn't lose interest in me, he just allowed me free control of my life for 65 years. He knew where I was whenever he wanted to rein me in; meanwhile he watched over and protected me until my 65th year of life, when He sent an *angel* to tell me the He needed me right then for something. The *angel* also told me that day that God promised that He would never forsake me or leave me.

I knew that the appearance of my dad that night was not a coincidence, nor an accident, but with everything going on, that he was an Envoy sent from God. If anyone would ever be in that position with God, it would be my Dad. I was still unsure of what the ultimate result would be. There was no doubt; this was more confirmation of whatever God was doing in my life. S had listened intently to me that night after we saw my Dad, and I noticed she was unusually quiet as I drove her home that night. I was not to see her again. Sheba and I drove back to the business, and I tried to get to sleep, but I felt such a strange loneliness. I slept very little that night, thinking about how knowledgeable my dad was, and how much I regretted never really knowing him better. I was eighteen when he died, and I squandered a lot of years when he was still alive. One day I will be able to tell him that, myself. S was the first employee, who had been allowed to see a real spiritual body at the business, of someone, who had died many years earlier. However, she would not be the last employee who would see my Dad, as well as the many other entities. I wasn't upset about my wife not being able to see the spirits, but it was that she didn't want to acknowledge that they even existed.

Sunday, July 10, would probably be kind of slow for business, since many locals went off to one of the area lakes on Sundays. S had been scheduled to work on Monday July 11, but her ex-boyfriend called me and told me that she got really scared Saturday night when my Dad had appeared. He told me that he knew that she wouldn't be back to work there. She had assured me when I hired her that she wasn't afraid of spirits. As it turned out S never even came back for some personal things she left at the store. I suppose she really was afraid, but I already knew that good spirits were the last thing that anyone needs to fear. That was why I had made plans to hire another model or two, so that I would not be shorthanded when one was out. I kept an ad running for attractive lingerie models, but I was quite selective on hiring. They had to provide several pictures, from which I would decide if they were a possibility. If that happened, first I would exchange an email dialogue, and if that was satisfactory, I would talk to them further on the phone and discuss the position. Then, I would I have them come in to the business for an interview. I wanted to watch their interest in customers, and the customer's response to them. Lastly, they could choose any lingerie piece or swimsuit in the store, which they would model for me, or for a customer who may be in the lingerie area. The entire process had worked well for a number of reasons, and it usually weeded out anyone who was not comfortable about the modeling aspect of the job. I had developed a sense of what it took for the applicant to make monies for herself, as well as the store. If they completed this process, then I could assure them that they would do well in the position, or else I would know that it would not work out. I would always be honest with the applicant, and if I promised her she would do well, she could count on it. I had a hiring ratio, of about one out of every seven applicants that applied. At that time, I had a young lady in Kansas, who I had been talking with the previous week, and she had an appointment to come in for an interview the next day Monday July 11. She appeared to be attractive, and also seemed to have a great personality, but her interview would determine if she was hired. Of all the personable applicants that I had interviewed, there was a sense, that I would hire this one, and yet I hadn't even met her yet. That would be perfect if it worked out like that, because I needed a new model that next week. Since it was Sunday, I decided I would close around 9 PM. Sunday was one of the days of the week, that I frequently closed early if business was really slow. Before I began locking up, I made the usual announcement that I was going to Grand Lake if anybody wanted to go. I was driving my four-door pickup that night, and it was filled with happy guests going to the lake with me. It was a beautiful clear summer night and my friends were in a festive mood. I could smell the odors of different varieties of alcohol, and cigarettes, in my truck. I had learned that weekends were celebrated in the spirit world, just as we do in the flesh body. That was another most interesting facet of my learning about the spirit world. The entities would usually ride all the way to the first entrance going into my farm. I would always tell them approximately what time I was going to leave the next day to go back to the store. Many of them would be back to my car early, and some would even make a point to let me know when they got back. Back when all of my riders were friendly ones, driving around with the entities in my vehicles, were like being part of a big happy crowd who were always excited. I can't tell you where they went after they got to my farm, but I assumed that they went anywhere they ever wanted to be. Imagine all the possibilities of going anywhere and for the most part being seen only by other spirits. That ability was what I believe fueled their excitement for the trips, and proves you really never know who is watching you. Whatever it was, they always seemed to be in such a happy mood and they were definitely still alive. I can tell you that on that particular trip, only a couple of them were back in my car the next morning so I must assume that they stayed longer. There were times that they would not come back with me to the store, but then I would see them later in the store that day. Evidently, they got back by some other means and I saw spirits get into customers cars at the store all the time. When the car drove away the spirits were in it and unless we knew the customer, we never told them that they had a passenger or maybe several passengers. I honestly saw a couple of males fairly often at the same time; leave the store in the afternoon at the so-called Happy Hour Times. I also saw them come back smelling of strong drink and being in a very happy mood. I can't explain it, but it was all a part of their spiritual mystique which never failed to amaze me. I saw many things that I never understood and that common experience was only one of those things. I had notified C Sunday afternoon that I would open the next day, and would stay for the evening shift as well. I would open the store at 8:30 AM, and J, the new model, was to be in by 5 PM. C was working less hours now, but I was giving her longer shifts, during the days that she worked. I knew that she was getting less hours, but I also knew that things may blow up at any time, particularly at night, if I wasn't there. I could see a real possibility that I may have to eventually stay there all the time. That was going to be very difficult, because I had lots of animals at the farm. My cattle were pretty much looked after by a neighbor, who also ran a few cattle on my farm. I had two older horses that I had for many years, and both of them were requiring more feeding, in addition to their pasture. Sometimes, I just didn't want to go home at night even though I was alone at the store, except for Sheba. Then there would come a time later, when I would not want stay at the store, but sure didn't want to make the long drive home either.

I opened Monday at 8:30 AM, and had an unusually busy Monday all by myself. The model applicant arrived right on time at 5 PM; being on time is a good start with me. The applicant, who I will call J, was personable and self assured. After talking a while, we had had several interruptions, with me checking out customers. So other than formalities, we had really discussed little about the position and the pay incentives. Of all of the models that I had hired, I had never hired one, without having them model something for me. J was obviously intelligent, and with a very laid back attitude. I decided that I had to bring the spirit issue up with her, since it looked like it was going to be an ongoing situation. After the basic conversation, I felt comfortable with her, and pretty much decided that I would offer her a position. That position would be dependent upon what her feelings were about the working environment. Without asking her to model anything, I said; "I need to ask you one important thing." She looked at me like she knew it was really serious. I ask her if she was afraid of spirits or ghosts of any kind. She without hesitating, said no she wasn't afraid, and quite calmly explained to me, why she was not afraid of them. Most job applicants would instantly think you were really weird, for asking such a question. We had a lot of laughs about that question, and it did sound really crazy. The problem was that it was a potential deal breaker, and I didn't want to waste time hiring another model that had such fears. I did realize that what I was seeking was quite rare, and that fact made me know that God had a strong hand in her hiring.

J told me of growing up with her grandmother, who had a Pre-1900 cemetery along an old wagon train route in southeast Kansas. J had had some pretty awesome experiences herself, involving spirits in those early childhood years. She later, after I hired her, told me that she knew what I was going to ask her that afternoon. I would've never believed that anyone could have imagined that normally, but this lady had a very psychic personality, like I had never seen. Then I asked another thing of her that I had never done at that time. I asked her if she wanted to start work that day, and she just smiled and said, sure. She was not asked to model anything before I hired her, I just knew she was exactly who I needed there. I was never more correct of my assessment of anyone, than of J, that July 11, 2011 afternoon. I had never hired anyone else in that manner, but I saw something in her that I felt would be a tremendous advantage to me. J brought more to me as an employee at that particular time, than I could have ever dreamed of.

She began work at 5:30 that day, and we hit it off so well. That was good, because everything is about to go up several levels right away. I knew nothing about Biblical numbers meanings at that time, but I would learn that the number *seven*, the date she started 7-11, the 7 meant **spiritual perfection.** That fact would prove to be so true within a few hours; maybe it was truly spiritual perfection. I would also learn that God's Timing is so important in everything he does for us. I know that after I hired J that afternoon, I felt a strong sense of relief, which I had not felt since the tornado on May 22. The visit from the *angel* as I referred to her, had given me a special attention to the events, which would come after the day she had visited. That date was June 25, and I would also learn that the number 25, in Biblical Terms, means **Double Grace.**

The afternoon and evening that J was hired, Monday July 11, 2011, was pretty busy with lingerie mostly. She did very well that evening in sales and modeling. I discovered that she was also very good with the computer. She was very busy until around 10:30 PM, then most of the customers began slowly clearing out. As business slowed, we sat in the office and I told her everything that was going on in my life. Only God could have understood what it meant to me, to finally have an understanding person listen to what was going on in my life. She understood my feelings so well, because she had gone through the exact thing when she was a very small child. Her experience had made a real mark on her. I was to learn how bad her experience had hurt her. It wasn't the same situation exactly, except that her parents could not accept the fact, that she was really seeing spirits and playing with them. The old cemetery along the wagon trail was less than 100 yards from her grandmother's home, and those children were from 150 years earlier. Her parents took her to psychologists for several years, and she was told weekly that spirits were not real. Finally, after observing J's parent's disbelief and not getting involved, on her deathbed, her grandmother told the parents that they had been wrong. She told them that she never wanted to get involved in their business, but that she knew J was playing with those good spirits for several years. She also told J's father, several days after his brother's death in Iraq, J had answered the phone, and it was her uncle who had been dead several days. J was overheard by her grandmother, talking to her uncle. J was now just 22 years old, and without her early exposure to the spirits, she would have never believed the story that I was telling her. However at the same time, I saw what the experience had created in that young vulnerable child by not believing her.

At that time, neither of us knew it, but J was about to join me in the early part of a most awesome journey. I would be introduced firsthand to God's Kingdom for the very first time in my life. Once I saw it, I knew that I wanted more of it. It became so very evident that God showed me those miracles, so that I would share them with others. I would promise God every night and day, that I would tell all who would listen what I had been shown. I would see the Evil of Satan like most people will never see nor believe. It would definitively confirm that Satan is just as real as we are, and he is also very powerful. I would see and battle with many of his chief soldiers. I would see and understand that our own government provides hands- on assistance to Satan by working daily with Satan's Army. Satan has disguised his army as some interesting form of exotic life, for thousands of years. With the help of our government for the last 65 plus years, his army has been crossbred and cloned into the most evil creatures that can be imagined. We would see firsthand who Satan has been gathering for thousands of years for that final battle. God would call it; The Battle of Good and Evil, and we are all involved in it on one side or the other. We would be exposed to solid living proof of our government's involvement with Satan, which has gone on for a very long time. Even though many things were being experienced the toughest encounters ever of my life were yet to come. Those encounters would be the proof which many will find hard to believe.

I was raised in a Christian home, where the Bible was taught. However, I didn't read the Bible, and knew little about anything religious, other than Easter and Christmas. The story of the Bible was so familiar to my father, but the biblical story and teachings, had very little interest to me. Like me, J had very little knowledge of the Bible as well, but together we were going to learn about our souls, and about the afterlife, in a most phenomenal way. Not a single automobile would ever appear in the parking lot, while teaching was in session. We also quickly learned the productions would never begin, until after we had locked up; no matter what time we actually closed. We could close early, but it would not begin until the building was locked up. Also, no one other than J and I, were ever allowed to witness what we were being shown. Nothing would record on the cameras while the productions were in progress. That night, we were sitting at the front counter, watching the set of nine monitors. I had already locked up the doors, and I planned to unlock the front door, to let J out when she left. I had turned off the outside lights except for the parking lot perimeter. Right at 11 PM, there appeared in the parking lot seven people; five men and two women. Each person standing in the parking lot appeared to have a bright light projecting down upon their head, similar to a portrait light. You could see all their faces as clear, as if they were only18 inches away. There was that number seven again, *seven people*, the men were two older and three younger. The two women were aged as the two men were, and were obviously their wives. It turned out that the three younger men were sons of the two older brothers and their wives. It would be the next day, before we would learn truly who they were. That night as would always be, no cars would come up into the front parking lot. We both realized that this was definitely a spiritual, religious event of some sort. All seven of the people stood in separate spots, throughout the front parking lot. None moved from their spots, until after we had closed up. It became nearly midnight, and I ask J if she needed to leave. She said that a neighbor always babysat for her, and if she was later than midnight getting home, she picked up the children at seven the next morning. She said the babysitter did not charge anymore for that. She told me that she would stay as long as I wanted to stay that night. We talked about who the entities may be, and why they were there in the parking lot, standing at semi attention. One older man was standing right in front of my truck, and the rest were probably 30 or 40 feet apart from each other. Another uncanny thing became evident, J had knowledge that I would've never thought of, about their manner of dress. It happened that her mother was actually from Germany, and J's father had married her while with the military in Germany. So J's grandparents, aunts, uncles, and cousins, all lived in Germany. She had visited them as she was growing up, and knew that the people in the parking lot were dressed in 1800-1900s German farm attire. She would be exactly correct about all the people being of German descent, I would learn the next afternoon. I already knew that the large farm adjoining my store on the east side was owned by a friendly, older man, who we will call Mr. B. His last name was quite commonly a German name, which had a slight change in spelling in this country. The way the people were standing in the parking lot, led us to believe that they were protecting us. They were each standing facing the building, but were frequently turning and looking back toward the interstate. It was so amazing to learn later, that some of these people had been dead more than 100 years, way before the highways, or automobiles were thought of. We had a feeling that their feelings for us were honorable. I told J that based on what we were seeing; I was going to invite them back the next night after closing, for a meeting. We talked about it a bit, and I unlocked the front door and walked outside.

I was able to see all of them face-to-face, as I stood directly in front of them outside the front door. I immediately realized that the oldest man looked very much like Mr. B, from the farm on the east side of me. I told them that I believed, they were members of the B family. They smiled as I talked to them, and I was sure that I was correct in who they were. I politely asked them if they would bring family members back to a meeting at the store, after closing at midnight the next night. The older men talked briefly with the wives, and they shook their heads yes, that they would come. I told them that hopefully we could answer questions for each other. At that time, I didn't understand that the spirit world has all the answers, and doesn't need to ask questions. I thanked them and went back inside to turn off the inside lights, and allow J out as well. She had been watching everything as it happened outside. We both felt like we were walking on clouds literally, after what we had just arranged. This would by far surpass anything that I had yet encountered in the spirit world, other than the *angel* coming to me with the Message from God. As J and I came out the door and locked it, the five people all turned and walked into the farm on the east side of my parking lot. Then as we watched, all five of them slowly disappeared into the late night mist. When that happened, it was like all of a sudden, the reality of what we were doing hit us simultaneously. We stood there five or 10 minutes in the parking lot, and J promised to be in by 4 that afternoon. Since it was close to 1:30 AM, we said good night. J went home, and Sheba and I went in and went to bed. Once again, I was stretched out in bed rehashing everything, and found it hard to get to sleep. As each event seemed to reach a new high, it was so very difficult to believe that all of this was really happening to me. Along with everything else that was going on I knew that J starting that day was not a coincidence, because there were too many things that she readily understood within the spirit world. I had been living within the spirit world for more than a month alone. Now I actually had someone with me, who understood all this every bit as well as I did. She not only understood things, but she was a strong quiet person who wasn't afraid of the entities that we were encountering. The mere fact that she wasn't uncomfortable with the spirits made it all much easier for me. The manner, in which J had come into this, just had to be another gift from God because the timing couldn't have been more right for me. When the *angel said; God was about to bestow a very special gift upon me,* she would be so right, better yet it would prove to be unlimited special gifts. She had also said; *He will do more than he promises.* That promise was just further proof that verifies that God's Hand was controlling every bit of it. However, I was also learning that when God gives us blessings, they usually have some strings attached. However, those strings are always something that will further heighten our relationship with God. Also, the gifts that He gives us can never be duplicated by anyone anywhere.

I finally went to sleep for maybe 4 hours, and I was up early, planning the night ahead already. It was Tuesday July 12, 2011, and I wanted to really try to find out what different things meant, that I had been seeing. I felt an indescribable anticipation for our meeting with the B family. It always seemed that Sheba would be just as excited as I would, as the events unfolded. It started out as a very slow day businesswise, so I had called C., and told her that she would not need to come in until Wednesday afternoon at 4 PM. I was going to try to allow C to work an occasional night every now and then. I had to go to my farm every few days at least. I knew that this schedule would change frequently, due to the number of hours I was putting in. I had no idea at that time, that God was about to begin showing nightly Biblical productions, beginning early the next week. This way, J could have off whenever I didn't work in the evening.

J came in at 4 PM, and was planning to stay that night as long as necessary. C had mentioned to her mother's friend about the number of spirits in the store. The friend was an older woman, who had been a member of a ghost hunters club for many years. C didn't know about the latest things, so all the friend knew about was the spirits in early June. Ironically, just before J got in at four, that lady had called me. She said C's mother had told her about the spirits in the store, and she thought maybe she might be able to help me. She told me how she had grown up going ghosts hunting with an aunt and uncle for years. Now she was involved with a local ghosts hunting group near Sarcoxie. After talking with her a few minutes, I decided I'd go ahead and tell her what had transpired the night before. She said that was very strange, what we had seen, and she had no idea what may be going on. She said as they were ghost hunting all those years, it was rare, if they ever saw more than one spirit every six months. She also told me that she had looked on the map of the area around my store, and that the B family cemetery was only 1/8 of a mile from my property, to the east. She didn't know that I had known Mr. B from the next door farm, for several years. I didn't dare tell her what was scheduled to transpire that night, because she had asked if I needed for her and her friends to come by sometime. I felt that it was much better to keep it as private as possible, to prevent upsetting the whole thing. The last thing I needed was a lot of publicity about what was going on. That was a good decision for now, but later things would change. I thanked her and told her I would call her if we needed her. I knew that this was a very special story that was developing in my life, and I sure didn't want to mess it up. Her story about the cemetery being near the store made a lot of sense to me. At that time, I still believed that people stayed in the graves after burial. I would later learn that usually only evil spirits hang around cemeteries. I would learn for a fact, that our spirits and souls go back to our Father the instant we die. Nevertheless, it made sense to J and I at the time, and added to our excitement for the evening. Even though now, I had 24/7 interaction with spirits, the meeting last night and tonight, was going to be with good people, who had been dead as long as 150 years. The afternoon and evening was a steady influx of customers coming and going. This was only the second day that J had worked, but she was doing very well. As the time moved on toward midnight, J and I could see and hear the invited guests coming in, through the back office which was always locked. This brought them into the area behind the counter, from there they went on into a back room. They were so considerate of not disturbing the business, there was no question they were good people. I believe that they began coming in at 11:30, because they knew that sometimes we closed early. We could hear them in the back office shuffling around. There was no doubt that they were just as excited about the meeting, as we were. They also understood that most people in flesh bodies would not participate in such a meeting. I had no doubt by then, that God was sanctioning the meeting, as part of His plan. I would later realize that it was definitely part of the teaching experience. As soon as it was midnight, we locked up the outside doors and turned off all the outside lights. Inside the building, I only left one small two bulb fluorescent on, and it was over the end of the counter. That way it was quite dark throughout the store, yet there was a faint glow behind the counter. As we planned earlier, J had taken her place inside my office door, directly behind the counter. She had a large monitor on the desk, where she could access all cameras inside the store, as well as throughout the parking lot. We left the office door open, which gave a slight additional light from the monitor. The plan was for her to be at the monitor, and to capture the images off of the monitor with her cell. I had also placed a voice recorder underneath the counter adjacent to where I was standing. The recorder was also just as close to the spokesman for the B family. What we did not realize at that time, was that the spirit voices may be very faint, and that a special extra sensitive recorder may be necessary. As I would find out after the meeting, only my voice would be heard during the meeting. The spirits voices were inaudible at best; only very light whispers in the recording. We didn't understand at that time, that even though the recorder was set in place before the people arrived, they would still know that it was there. If they didn't want to be recorded that would explain the soft voices. Later in the meeting they would speak loudly enough for us to understand them. If I had been able to actually record their voices during that meeting, it would have probably been at first ever. Although, quite possibly God never intended for them to be recorded. Many times I tried to take pictures of certain scenes, and the frame would become covered with a Red mesh blur instantly. I had learned that certain things were not going to be allowed to be photographed. We would be able to secure two pictures of the older Mr. B at the end of the meeting, as we shook hands. At five minutes after midnight, J was still behind the counter with me and had not gone into the office yet. While we could tell there were a lot of people in the store lobby, we could still hear many in the library. I told J that I was going into the library to escort the remaining people out to the front. It was a very strange feeling, as I went down the hallway in pitch darkness into the library. The library was an 18 x 16 room that was very dark when all the lights were off. I introduced myself to the guests, and told them if they were members of Mr. B's family, that our meeting was about to start. I turned around and walked back out into the store, as they followed directly behind. That itself was a quite eerie feeling, hearing the farm boots of the men scuffing the floor as they walked behind me. I could hear them whispering to each other within two feet behind me. It appeared there had been probably 8 to 10 people in the back room that followed me out. I noted that the same three young men, who had been in the parking lot the night before, were the first to follow me out. The three of them took their places against the wall, almost directly underneath the small lighted florescent. It was an awesome feeling, seeing the three tall young men standing side-by-side very straight against the wall. Very respectfully they had taken off their black hats and were holding them with both hands down in front of them. They all three wore heavy black work boots, black pants and very white shirts. All three had dark hair and it was cut short, and all of the men's faces were cleanly shaved. The young men were within 5 feet of where I would be standing, behind the counter. Directly across the counter and facing me was the obvious older of the two brothers, who was the spokesman for the group. I could not help but be amazed, at how much he resembled the slight built Mr. B at the farm. It appeared that the older gentleman facing me was an exact duplicate of Mr. B, except that he was even thinner in stature than Mr. B. I still had a strong feeling that he was Mr. B's grandfather. J was to take two legible pictures of the older brother, which would confirm that he was Mr. B's grandfather. To his right side facing me was his wife, and to her right, were the other brother and his wife. I felt that they all presented themselves in varying ages, was so that I would be able to verify my story with their close relative, Mr. B. Standing in the store lobby were probably another 20 to 30 people that we could see, but not identify. The store lobby area was 1600 ft., and it looked like it may be half full of people either standing or leaning against the glass cases. [2] Those people had no obvious part in the meeting other than observing.

I told J to take her place in the office, and I again introduced J and myself, by our full names. It wasn't as if they didn't already know who we were, but I felt that I would err on the side of sincerity. I then said to them;" I really want to thank all of you B family members for being here tonight". I told them that as they knew, the meeting was for the understanding of everyone, and so that we may be able to cooperate in everything that was to transpire. I told them that as they likely knew, lots of beautiful things had been happening in my life. I explained that so far most everything had been pleasant, but that we all knew the evil would become involved at some point. So, I asked them to join me in a Prayer to God, in order that we may ask Him for power against those who may be agents of Satan. The intent was to allow us to prevent evildoers from entering into our meeting group. I could see that they were all shaking their heads yes, even the unknown persons in the audience. I had a strong feeling that they were all religious people. I explained to all of the family again, that I knew and respected Mr. B the farmer next door. At that point, I took the liberty to tell them how much he resembled some of them in front. There was little doubt that the two older brothers were exactly, who I believed they were. They were Mr. B's Grandfather, and the other brother was his Great Uncle. I had learned from the" ghost hunter lady" that the B family had evidently been well respected, when they left Germany and came to America. I again saw a lot of smiling faces when I made that statement to them. I began explaining to them how I would like to know what they knew about the events that were happening in my life. Of course, as spirits, they knew everything, but I didn't understand that yet.

I had begun to see that whenever I had direct interaction with an entity, I would usually get an understanding of their thoughts about me. I was also beginning to read their thoughts when they looked at me. Before the night would end, I would learn from the B family that God was behind the things happening in my life. Without discussing it with anyone for a couple of weeks, I had been quietly testing what I thought was correct. I had two friendly entities that were present much of the time in the store. I began a nightly dialogue with them about all sorts of subjects. Because of that interaction, I was much better at understanding what the entities projected thought wise to me. The vast majority of the spirits conversations with others are enacted merely by ESP. Later, I was to later learn that many of the evil entities from outer space are supernaturally powerful. Firsthand, I would see and feel those evil ones causing real hurt upon me and my dogs. I would learn that the human entities possessed much lower paranormal ability than the outer space entities. Yet as the spiritual bodies that we become after death; we do have lots of strengths that we do not have in physical bodies. I will be able to elaborate much more on this subject later in the story, because I was to become much more educated over the next year and a half. The B family appeared early in the lessons, *as* representatives of God, and I believe they were used to confirm that the *angel* visit two weeks earlier was for real. I would later understand that the four B family members were Saints from God, who were sent to help me through the trials that I was going to encounter. A number of other helpers in spiritual bodies would also present themselves in crucial times. There were three other people in Spirit Forms, who I also saw as Saints of God. One was a young Indian Chief from the 1800's, another was My Dad, and the Third was a very small man who reminded us of a Leprechaun. He was not much more than three feet tall, and once was dressed similar to pictures I've seen of Leprechauns, including the top hat. He was present from early after the Joplin Tornado, and for more than two years afterward. There are several clear pictures of that "little man" in different areas of the building, but mostly in the front parking lot. He would usually appear at night, and he preferred rainy nights. A Cherokee Medicine Man who became my friend, was another who God used to help me through a particularly perilous time, I will call him S. He told me that the Cherokee's were taught as children, that the appearances of the "little people" always represented good luck that was to come.

As I continued speaking to the B family, I related with them about my tornado experience, and it was evident they knew all about it. They knew all about the spirits appearing four days after the tornado. Suddenly it hit me; they knew everything that was to come as well. J came out of the office about that time, and she handed me a note, that she gotten a clear picture of the older Mr. B. I motioned for her to go back into the office until I adjourned the meeting, and that there may be another great picture opportunity. We had definitely determined that the family was there to help us through the trials and tribulations, which we knew were coming. It was so beautiful to watch them as they reacted to things we said, and to questions we asked of them. Sheba was always so happy to be around the good entities, and that night was no exception. They would occasionally pat her head, when they came around her, and her nubby tail was wiggling.

Finally, I realized that it was nearly 3:00AM. I told them how grateful we were to everyone for coming, and I promised them I would do everything I could to justify their faith in me. I asked if anyone had anything else to discuss. The perceived patriarch, Mr. B, was nodding his head, that they had no further questions. I knew that there was much more that we didn't know, but felt that it was going to be disclosed as we went forward. I stuck my head around my office door, and told J to get ready for a picture. Then, I looked directly at the senior Mr. B and thanked him personally. Then as other three next to him looked on, I reached over the counter and shook his hand. I heard J say" he just shook your hand." That was such an awesome feeling, and I heard J again say excitedly," Lynwood, I just got a picture of him shaking hands with you." She was now behind me and couldn't wait to show me that picture. As everyone in the store area began shuffling out through rear locked door, I noticed the four in front hadn't left the building. A fifth person had joined them, and they disappeared all at once. While we were wondering where the five had gone, we began hearing strange voices somewhere in the building. J and I went to several different locations within the store building, but no single location seemed to give us any better understanding of their ongoing discussion. Finally, we decided that the back office was as good as any to hear from so we sat down there. Since my hearing in one ear had been damaged long ago, I was unable to understand the soft female voices, but between the two of us we could determine that they were in a discussion of some subject. I could hear the men and women well enough to realize that they were speaking in a German or Dutch language. At that moment Jessica said to me that they were speaking German, and it hit me that J had said her mother was from Germany. She told me that she would try to explain to me what they were taking about as best she could. That temporary language barrier would be further proof of God's role, in His timing for bringing J into my employment. Additionally, it had been the newly hired J, who had recognized that the people were dressed in 18ᵗʰ century German farm attire when they first appeared the night before. It seemed the five people were deciding if I was the right person for some job that they were discussing. They were voting on my qualifications for that specific job. Their initial discussion lasted for maybe ten minutes, and all but the one oldest woman had thought that I was the right one for the job. We had no idea what the job was, but we assumed that it had to be whatever it was, that the *angel* had said God needed me to do. They all had different reasons that they thought I was worthy of the position. One of the older women, who we believed was the sister in law of the older Mr. B, just wasn't quite sure if I was the right choice for that position. It seemed though that the 5ᵗʰ younger woman had convinced her otherwise, and after maybe 20 minutes more of discussion they decided unanimously that I was the person, who they referred to as "the right one for it."At that point we heard them leave the building exactly the way that the first group had left. They seemed totally oblivious to J and I overhearing their discussion. We felt that they certainly had wanted us to hear them, because their voices were audible, unlike the almost three hours meeting beforehand. That led us to believe, that they had purposely spoken very quietly early in the meeting, because they knew that we were attempting to record their voices. While we never heard "it" clarified, J and I had no doubt that the plan was from God, and that the B family were an important part as well. However, we still had no inkling as to where it would all lead. I knew that I didn't feel deserving of all the awesome things that were happening in my life. I had always used that excuse; *that I couldn't ever please God, and that he sure wouldn't take me like I was,* as an excuse not to change. I now know for a fact that there are many millions of us who use that same excuse. I was going to learn in so many of the most miraculous ways how God will help us conform and grow closer to Him at the same time. God will teach you how to develop faith in Him beginning with easy situations, which will definitely strengthen your faith in Him.

After I finally begin learning the Bible more than a year after these events, I would learn a Bible Passage where God would tell Moses; That He would choose whomever He wished for His Purposes. So today; *I am living proof that God will take you as flawed as you may be, and He will mold you into the person that you are to be.* I do now realize that God has a plan for all of us, but like I did, most of us ignore certain opportunities when they appear. J along with me would be witness to many more unbelievable spiritually events that year. She would also see many of the entities in the building, the parking lots, and even her own car. They were as horrifying as the creatures in any outer space being film. As for myself, I knew that I was slowly changing the way that I reacted to things that were happening. While my life was changing for the better, I would still find lots of obstacles along the way, and it would be a long time before I would understand where all this was going. It had been a most unbelievable two nights; and we were to see more of the B family again and soon. Little did we know but within several more days I was to see my dad again, and it would the second time within a two week period. In addition to that, what we would call the Bible teaching was going to be taught to us over a several night period. J and I would often tell people that Hollywood couldn't have produced anything more beautiful than or as realistic as those visions were. They were always in beautiful color with real life spirits that appeared as real as we were. They were played out in the parking lots and adjacent field and woods around the store. J and I looked forward every night for what was coming up next. When we would see scenes that we didn't understand, either one of us would always say that we wondered what something meant. Then even if I only got had hours sleep, I would wake up knowing the answer to whatever we had wondered about. That is still one of the main ways with which God answers my concerns about something in my life today. I will wake up and it will be like I talked to someone who answered my concern. That answer comes from God, and anyone can have that same experience with Him.

Within a day or two, I began thinking seriously about whether it was right to tell Mr. B about the experience we shared with his family. That was a decision that would have to wait for a couple of months, before I made up my mind. I probably would someday sit down with him and fully relate what had transpired on July 11 and 12, 2011. I wanted to discuss it with his son-in-law before I decided. I felt that his relatives from one- hundred plus years ago would never truly leave us, until everything in the plan had been completed. Little did I know, but everything would go on for a long time, only the location would occasionally be moved. As the months went by and situations became more difficult, rarely were there times when I didn't still feel the presence of that family.

It was now 3:45 AM, on Wednesday July 13, 2011. J and I were exhausted but feeling giddy from all that we had encountered in two nights. We looked at the pictures she had taken from the camera monitor. There I was shaking hands over the counter, with a man who had died more than one-hundred years ago. We sat and talked until nearly 5:30, and I hugged J Good Night, even as daylight was breaking in the East. At least she could sleep that day after she got home, but at best, I would have two hours if I went right to sleep. She left and Sheba and I went back inside and went to sleep. We radio was usually set for 7AM, but I had forgot to turn the alarm on. Sheba and I had overslept until 8:30 that morning, and I woke up still on Cloud 9 from the night before. I had only a total of two and one-half hours sleep, and the night before had maybe five hours at best. It had still been a most exciting 48 hours for us. Those days it seemed like it was one event after another, and they were all coming closer together. Each event was progressively becoming more spiritually meaningful, but I would eventually find myself alone in many of the encounters ahead, if it were not for my beautiful Sheba. It was Wednesday July 13, and J would be in that afternoon by 6. C was coming in at 9:30AM, and I was going to my farm in Oklahoma for several hours to catch up on chores. I planned to be back to the store by 6PM. as well.

Wednesday afternoon, J and I both got to the store just about the same time. I had updated my wife about the Monday and Tuesday night events that we had been involved in. I had gotten the usual no comments or questions reply from her. Old habits were going to be very hard for me to break, but for forty years we had told each other everything. Now the most special things that a man could ever tell his family, was falling on deaf ears because of my wife's decision to disbelieve me. That night was pretty slow until 11 and I let J off to go home early. I had arranged with C that I would to stay overnight and work the next morning, and she would work from 4PM until closing. Since the *angel's* appearance on June 25th, I had remembered what the old pastor had said about watch out for evil spirits appearing at some point. I began praying to God, asking Him if we were getting too deep into the spirit world with our interactions. God would always let me understand with clear feelings that I just had to be very careful, so as not to attract evil spirits. I definitely knew that God wanted me to learn all I could about the spirit world. I had no idea why, and it would be a long time before I would actually know why. We had learned that the males in the red, yellow and blue outfits were evil persons, and that they were there for some specific learning experience. That night I closed at 11:30 and Sheba and I went to bed. In my bedroom at the store, I had a lot of storage area in the rear of my sleeping area. I had some heavy, blue plastic shelving material that was packaged together into 50 pound blocks. The blocks of shelving were stacked at the foot of my double bed, and beside the bed was another double size mattress that was leaning sideways against the wall. The narrow width of that mattress was along the floor, and slid only along on the edge. I hadn't mentioned it to anyone; but the last several nights that I had slept there, something was sliding that mattress slowly back and forth all night along the floor. The mattress probably weighed 75 pounds and it was being slid alongside between the wall and my bed. I knew that there were a lot of entities inside the building, but they hadn't been causing any real problems thus far. That night was no different, and whatever it was continued as usual throughout the night sliding the mattress. Usually our guests always seemed to go out of their way to avoid causing a problem, but that next morning I was awakened by loud radio music. The radio sounded like it was up in my attic, but when I got up it seemed like it was coming from another area. It was before 7 AM when I usually would be awakened by my own radio, so it was an unusual happening. These events as well as the mattress pusher as I began calling him were the early signs of some evildoers. I went up front and unlocked the doors and let Sheba out into the parking lot. It was Thursday morning July 14, and I was going to work until 4 in the afternoon when C would be in. That afternoon when C got in at 4, I told her that if she wanted to make more hours for that week, I had an idea. She said that she wanted to be off all day Saturday for something if possible. So I ended up letting her work that night and the next day, Friday July 15 until 4PM, and she could then be off until Sunday afternoon at 5PM. That way I would be able to go home and stay until Friday afternoon before coming back to the store, but would work all weekend until Sunday afternoon. I had notified J earlier that she could take off Thursday night since I was not going to be working either. She would then come in to work Friday at 4, and also would work Saturday from 3PM until closing. Friday afternoon, I got a call from J that her little boy had been sick all day, and that she needed to stay with him that night. If he was better she planned to come in by 3 Saturday afternoon. My night was interesting since I had a couple that I knew pretty well came by to visit on their way to Springfield. They both knew about the spirit happenings in the store, and the three of us sat and watched some unusual things that evening on the monitors. The couple both in their 40s had been jokingly discussing the wife doing some modeling of lingerie while in the store. I had employed models of different ages at times, and one of the models in her late 40s had done quite well while selling lingerie for us. That night we had two ladies in the 40-50 age range shopping for a swim suit for one of them. As it happened, the couple that was visiting offered to demonstrate the wife's modeling and sales ability. She ended up selling both of the women lingerie, plus the swim suit that they had originally came in looking for. Hence, she earned some income while doing something that made her feel good about herself. My friends were so enthused about the wife's ability, I later employed her for a few days when I was short an employee. I walked my friends out to their car at midnight, and Sheba and I sat outside while I smoked a cigar that someone had left me. We went inside and got to bed around 1:30AM. As I began looking at the overnight camera log the next morning, I saw that there had been lots of crazy stuff on the cameras. It was July 16, 2011 and J was to call me if her little one wasn't feeling better. Instead she did text me while Sheba and I were driving up to the convenience store, and said that her little boy was feeling better and she would be in by 3. That morning Sheba was in one of her more playful modes, even before she had gotten me to wake up. So when we got back to the store I put her on the front outside chain because she was feeling so energetic. She really needed more exercise anyway, so I often would leave her out for short periods of time right underneath a front camera. There would come a time later when I didn't want her to get out of my sight.

Sheba seemed so happy in the mornings wiggling her nubby tail, and bouncing around like a bucking bull. Sheba had become my very best friend since the tornado, and it seemed that our mutual experiences were bonding us tightly. I had gotten Sheba from two older ladies in Carthage, Missouri in early September 2010. I had owned a number of very good Rottweiler's over the previous 20 years. Strangely enough, I began looking for a really well bred female in August 2010. I found an ad in the paper advertising a four-year-old Rottweiler female for sale in Carthage. I kept the ad in my office for a week or so, before I called about the Rottweiler. I talked to an older lady who told me that the dog was very intelligent, and that they had to get rid of her. She said that she and her mother had to move into an assisted living facility in Arizona, and they were not allowed to have pets there. They were looking to find a really good home for her. I told her that I would call back to make an appointment to see the dog. Another two weeks or so went by, before I called and made an appointment to go see her dog. Ironically, it was September 7 when I went to Carthage to see Sheba for the first time. Once again that *number seven* showed up. I mentioned earlier, that I had never known anything about Biblical meanings of numbers, until probably more than two and one-half years after 2011. Once I began diligently learning the Bible; I saw a number of examples of Biblical prophecies showing up in my experiences, which officially began with the tornado. I went back at some point then, and began looking at the reams of almost daily notes that I had kept

since 2011. I had begun keeping pretty detailed notes on Saturday May 28, 2011. That was the day after the blue lines had changed to human forms on the outside cameras. It would also later that evening, when my friends would first witness the spirits around the outside doors. Sheba would turn out to be the greatest dog that I have ever owned. I have owned several intelligent Rottweiler and Dobermans in my life, so that is an extraordinary compliment to her. I wanted a Rottweiler to keep at the store, since I only worked women in the business. I had the first manager who had been a male, and he made a real mess of the business. I began hiring all females shortly after he was terminated in early 2007. I had since hired one more male employee who was very unsatisfactory as well. So I made a policy in 2008 that I would only hire females, and it has worked well. I believe that having in the store may cut down on the potential for robbery. I went over to Carthage to see the Rottweiler, and I was met at the door by Sheba and the younger of the two women. Sheba seemed to have her eyes on me constantly, as we walked into the living room. I was introduced to the older of the ladies, probably well in her 70s and seated in a wheelchair. Her daughter who I had been talking to was probably in her 50s. The younger lady who was doing most of the talking stood beside her mother in the wheelchair. Sheba sat down to the left of the younger woman, and she was facing me. She never seemed to take her eyes off of me. I could immediately tell that she was a very intelligent, just by her interest in everything I was doing. The younger lady began telling me that they had had Sheba most of her adult life, since she was around one year old, and they had gotten her from a lady in Kansas City. They believed that she was currently 4 years old and she had had only one litter of pups. They began asking me questions about what I intended to do with Sheba, and I knew they were being very careful about who they sold her to. They wanted to make sure that she had a very good home, because she meant a lot to them. After talking with them for maybe half an hour, Sheba was still looking at me intently. I realized that I was going through an application process for a dog, but it all made sense afterwards. Sheba would prove without a doubt, to be another special gift from God. He had planned out everything well ahead, and He knew that within eight months, I would truly begin appreciating her. The younger lady said to me, that they believed Sheba would have a good home with me. I promised them that I would take very good care of her, and that I would never get rid of her. As I made that statement to the ladies, Sheba looked up at the younger lady beside her, and then to the older lady in the wheelchair. The younger woman hugged Sheba's neck, and then led her over to the wheelchair. With great effort, the older woman was able to reach her arms around Sheba's neck and hug her. Sheba then got up and walked over to my right side and sat down facing the women. At that point she knew that she was about to leave them. I had never seen anything like that in my entire life with animals; and that process had further convinced me of her intelligence. I shook hands with both of the women and gave them my toll-free cell phone number. They didn't know what their phone number would be in Arizona, but said they would call me after they got moved. Although I never heard from them ever again, and I have wished a lot of times that I had been able to explain all the wonderful things Sheba did for me, before her death on early April Morning in 2015. Ironically, Sheba eventually died from injuries that she had received that April morning in 2012 while protecting me from aliens in my bedroom at the store A part of my heart went with her that beautiful Easter Morning at Sunrise when she died. Knowing everything that Sheba had witnessed and was attacked by, I believe with all my heart that God the Father took her into his arms at that beautifully appropriate time because Sheba was one of *His Angels*. The one real consolation that I have is my knowing without a doubt, that one day she will be reunited with me forever. After things had gotten bad at the Missouri location, I always half kiddingly told my employees that one day they would see me, Sheba, and Beau my black male who was raised by Sheba, in Heaven. Sheba was injured in an incident that was like something directly out of a Star Wars movie scene, and she would slowly begin suffering a sickening demise. She like me would have a massive cancer inside her body. Sheba was rolling me over that morning trying to wake me as the aliens inserted four holes into the top of my head. The two identical entities that injured her with a highly sophisticated star wars type weapons were definitely extra terrestrials, and I would later understand through discernment from God, that those two creatures were directly from the authority of Satan. I wished many times that I could have contact from Sheba's former owners. I never had an occasion to know for sure, but then I believed that those two women were Christians. Sheba always seemed to have an understanding of the things that were going on in, far above what most dogs could comprehend. I would have truly loved to tell the nice old ladies what an awesome asset in my life that Sheba became. As things would become much tougher in all the events to come, Sheba would be my most trusted friend. She never left my side night or day, and never even wanted to be outside of a closed door if I was on the inside. That was her way of protecting me, and there would be lots of times she would face some pretty powerful enemies up close. Sheba was the only dog that ever taught me about things, that humans don't normally understand. She taught me how to ascertain instantly between good and evil spirits, and she would have a facial expression that reflected the differences.

Since she died, I have thought many times of, how much she only wanted to be with me, beginning the instant I took her away from her former owners. The day that I got her, she had jumped up into the front seat of my truck and sat like a person in the seat. All the way back to the store, she was looking at me frequently. It was my plan on September 7, 2010 when I got her, that she would live with A the model, who had just moved into the home behind the store. Sheba would then be either with A at the house or in the store all the time. That way she would be good protection against robberies and break-ins. Then each night after closing, I would walk A and Sheba over to the house. I began noticing that Sheba would hang back with me as we approached the house. Then as we walked up on the porch, she did not want to walk into the house without me. This became a nightly ritual, with A calling me after I left, telling me how upset Sheba became whenever I left. I tried to disregard it, but A was constantly telling me that Sheba was even getting sick and throwing up, even chewing up the carpet when I left her. In hindsight, I know for a fact that God had intended Sheba to be with me all the time. I believe that He wanted Sheba and me to bond well before May 22, 2011, the day of the tornado. As it worked out, A would be leaving on December 10, 2010, and Sheba and I would then be together 24/7. While we were to have many beautiful times together, I truly regret my decision to leave Sheba for those three months in 2010. After the tornado on May 22, there seemed to be few times that we would ever enjoy total serenity, without something unpleasant in the mix. Without a doubt, I know that had I not her, I could not have survived those times, when things became too tough for almost everyone. It is my solid belief that God well knew the dangerous and lonely times that were ahead, when He encouraged me to go and see Sheba on September 7, because He knew that once I saw her, I would definitely want her. Then there came a day in April 2012 that she would without a doubt, save my sanity and probably my life as well. I was in contact with a very capable medical doctor within minutes after Sheba's actions. Based on his detailed information concerning the enemies who I had encountered, I certainly felt that her intelligent timely reaction was authorized by God's Own Hand that day. The events of that most awful event were forever etched into the beautiful memory of my Sheba. Someone who understands dogs would know that since Sheba always owned only by women, she would not have immediately accepted a male owner. With all the many remarkable things that she did for me, in addition to her instant bonding with me, seems to have guaranteed that God had brought her into my life to help keep me alive.

It was Saturday morning July 16, 2011, and J would be in by 3 that day. I had bought a couple of slices of breakfast pizza at the store. I gave her a half of a slice on the way back to the store. I had bought a large cup of their coffee at the convenience store. It usually tasted much better than what we made in the store. I kept dry feed out for Sheba all the time, and she ate it whenever she wanted it, but she always wanted some of whatever I was eating. It began like a normal Saturday with business slow, but steadily picked up pretty much all day. J made it in that afternoon at 2:45 and planned to work until midnight. After she got to work in the afternoon, the lingerie business was pretty good well into the evening until 10. As we sat down in the office, I told her that she could leave at 11:30 if the business was still slow at that time. She and I began watching the store cameras on my office monitors. Those days we were seeing all kinds of things happening late at night. It was like you never knew what you were going to see next, and it was quite entertaining to watch the entities in their activities. Just before 11:30, J got up to go to the dressing area in the lingerie section of the store. All of a sudden, it was exactly as the previous Saturday night July 9th at 11:30PM, when the last model was working. Jessica was at the counter's main monitor and screamed out to me; "Lynwood, there is a little man at the front door who's dressed like 1960." Just as the week before to the minute, I looked at the monitor on my desk. I said." it is my Dad J, just like last Saturday night that I told you about and even at the same time." I ran around the counter as I saw my Dad standing at the front door, again looking up at the Red Adult Open Sign. Again, we both ran out the door, and of course he was gone, and there was not a single car in the parking lot. Each time I had seen him looking up at that sign, I knew that I was being gently chastised for owning that adult business. It had to be, that because of all my interactions with the spirits, I had become able to pretty well decipher the thoughts that were being transmitted to me. My Dad was only about five feet and six inches tall, but he always had been able to could get his ideas across to me without whippings. There was no doubt about it, the adult business sign was not meeting my Dad's approval one bit and he was telling me that. What was so amazing about him appearing again this time, were the similarities to the first time; he appeared in the exact place, he appeared on the same day of the week, he appeared at precisely the same time, and a different girl saw him this time, but yet she yelled the exact same phrase. There was another very important thing, the Biblical number Seven; he had both times appeared in the Seventh month, and his appearances were Seven Days apart. Biblically, the number Seven means Spiritual Perfection. There were now two different people who had actually seen my Dad, and he had been gone from this life more than Forty-Seven years. I was to again see my Dad appear in July 2012, but he would look really obviously pleased with me by that time.

That night J and I we went ahead and locked up at midnight, but we both went back inside to talk about the latest event. We both were amused that with all the similar occurrences, J had even yelled out the exact thing as the girl had one week earlier. The "dressed like 1960" is the lyric in a David Allen Coe tune called Midnight in Montgomery, about country singer legend Hank Williams Sr. We always were able to see the monitors from wherever we sat in the office or at the counter. It was so very amusing to watch them in those times, and it was becoming more so with every passing day. Sometimes when business was slow and we began watching the cameras, some of those I referred to as good entities, enjoyed performing dress shows for us. They would sometimes pretend to get really dressed up and have a wedding. Sometimes they would start playing and chasing each other throughout the store, and would be knocking items off the racks unintentionally. There were all sorts of possibilities that they could choose from, but they were all decently entertaining. J sat with me for maybe two hours before leaving. The next day was Sunday and she was to be off all day, so she talked about sleeping in the next morning. Sheba and I walked her out to the car with her, we said good night and she left. Sheba and I went in locked the front door and went to bed. It had been a third unbelievable night in less than one week, I was so very thankful that I had someone with me during those nights. J would fortunately for me, be a witness to some of the most bizarre sights and happenings that anyone could ever imagine. Even though she had only been working with me six nights, she had already been a part of some of the most awesome happenings yet. She always just smiled if someone asked her about any of the unbelievable things that we had seen. She would then describe to them the things we had been seeing, and she would always be so calm and unemotional about explaining everything. I will always know that J was sent to me at the exact time period that she appeared, for some specific reason which only God knows. After finally beginning to understand many things that happened, I most definitely believe that one day God will call on J for something important in his plans. He spent lots of effort and timing to show and teach us two sinners a lot of Biblical understanding. I knew that God was intervening in my life, but I also believe He was intervening in J's as well; it just might be awhile before she realizes it. No matter what is to come in her life, certainly God knows how much support that she provided to me in that period of my life. Since I know for a fact that God orchestrated everything that we witnessed, I believe that J will be rewarded for her input during those times. I was going to leave the next day at 4PM when C would be coming in, and I would be off until Monday afternoon. I was going to try to get some badly needed rest if possible. I had no idea how much I would need that rest, because we didn't know that Monday night another event was going to be. As in everything thus far, each event would progressively become more spiritually powerful, and the next week's events would be no different. I finally went to sleep that night and got a good night's rest. Sheba and I got up early and drove the four miles over to Sarcoxie that morning for some breakfast. By the time I got back and unlocked all the doors it was 8:45AM. Sundays were usually pretty busy sales days during the summer, since lots of people drove to the lakes on Sunday. If they didn't stop on the way over, they would sometimes stop on the way back that evening. Summer was also vacation time and lots of out of state customers stopped. That Sunday, the 17th of July was a fairly average day with nothing unusual happening up until when C came in at 4 that afternoon. I sat down and told her in more detail about the three events that had transpired since J had begun working. She had her mother, who knew that the spirits were real because she was able to see pictures. Yet somehow C and her boyfriend weren't quite sure about it all even though she knew well that I was an honest person. I have had my share of flaws, but dishonesty has not been one of them. However there would come a time when C was working at night, when I would see images the next day from the cameras as she was leaving, and I would see that she was taking pictures of the inside of her car before she got into it. She had seen me doing that from the start. I felt that it was likely my wife was also telling her that I was having delusions; and I knew that C didn't want to get crossed up with my wife on anything she said. I was usually more even tempered and I didn't usually rush to judgment unless it was a life or death decision. I definitely wouldn't fire someone merely because they couldn't see what I was seeing. My wife had always kept a tight relationship with C through control and C definitely feared losing her job. She would eventually realize that there was truth to the things that I was seeing, because the store cam pictures were beginning to accumulate. Several of my future employees would be harassed by my wife until they quit, particularly if they were also seeing the entities. Her attempts to discredit me were beginning to cause some potentially serious conditions in my life. Later those false accusations against me would truly develop into some monumental life events for my entire family. I left to go to my farm and I planned to get some rest before coming back in Monday at 5.

Monday afternoon July 18 was a muggy afternoon as I drove to work. I had mowed a large portion of my rather large yard at home that morning, and was kind of hoping for a quiet night. C had told me about a lingerie order that came in that afternoon, and it had to all be catalogued, labeled and priced as early as possible. Then we had to get multiple pieces of everything out on the racks as early as possible. It was one of the chores in retail sales that I never liked, but it was necessary. When J got in at 5:30 I had her to start separating the lingerie pieces out for us to begin processing. We worked on the inventory all evening while also taking care of normal customer needs. At 11PM we noticed on the outside cameras, what appeared to be several beautiful crystal colored lights that were very white in color in several places in the parking area. I went out with my digital camera and took pictures of one of the larger lights that were nearest to the building. The instant the camera took it; the picture began developing a red mesh over the image until the image was covered, and then it disappeared completely. I tried several more pictures with the same result. I even walked out across the pasture fence on the east side onto the B farm, and took a picture of one of the beautiful crystal lights in the edge of some large trees. I had the same result as the other pictures; the red mesh appeared and dissolved the image. This was an event that would be repeated many times over the next two years. The lesson learned was that God would absolutely not allow certain images within His Kingdom to be photographed under those circumstances. For that same reason, my store cameras could not develop or save an image of certain people or things that were not allowed. It would also be the same results with our cell phones. Only God would have objected to the pictures of those certain subjects and I instantly understood that, and for the most part I quit trying to photograph questionable things. There were times when I saw such unbelievable photo potentials that I would still try once on them. After that I would always promise God that I would not try that particular object again. On September 25, 2011, I actually took a very clear picture of Satan outside of my store building leaning against a 500-gallon propane tank at 5:30 AM., just as daylight was breaking. The picture took and to my astonishment, I would constantly keep looking at it that morning after taking it, because I was so pleasantly surprised that it was still visible. I had used my cell phone and the picture was saved on my phone. I was on Cloud 9, but so anxious to get it copied as soon as C or J got in to work. I had a distinct fear that it would disappear before I could get it duplicated, so I constantly checked and rechecked my cell for the picture. Sure enough around 9:30AM, I tried to check the picture for what seemed like the 100th time, and that unbelievable image of the Devil himself had clearly disappeared. That clear picture of a bedraggled, almost beaten Satan leaning against the large propane tank was completely gone. That afternoon I had my cell phone and pictures examined by a couple of knowledgeable individuals and they could find no trace of that image. I concluded that God always put the red mesh covering over certain images, in order to prevent anyone being able to expose certain things within His Kingdom. Satan knew that I had taken his clear picture at 5:30 that morning, showing him in an obvious weakened appearance. Then Satan with his usual arrogance, and forever wanting to emulate Jesus, then attempted to erase that image in the same manner that God erased images. However Satan found himself barred from using the color Red, and was delegated to the color Black. The color Red Biblically is the most meaningful and symbolic color in all of Scripture. In stark contrast, the color Black Biblically, symbolizes darkness as is Satan's official title, the Prince of Darkness. That entire incident was neither an accident nor coincidence, but was God actually beginning the task of exposing Satan's methodical powers to me. I had been allowed to understand only a basic example of the ingenuity of Satan. I would learn to recognize his powers that are trying to influence our lives daily. I would gain a strong sense of how to be attuned to the things Satan does to corrupt our thoughts. However, even though I was being shown so dramatically all those examples of good and evil, I was still far from being one of the good.

That night we closed officially at midnight, but after we locked up J and I sat down at the counter. We knew that something else big was starting up, but did not understand the beautiful shimmering crystal white lights. There was one light the along the west parking lot, one in the front east corner lot, and the one over on the B farm across the fence. As we were watching the lights, we saw that a crystal light was being erected as we watched. It was being built on the side of J's compact white car that was parked in front of the store, but one space east of the front entrance. Once again we found that the image was coming through live on the cameras but was not being recorded. We went outside the front door and were within 10 feet of the car and the light, and again I tried to take a picture. As the image began to be enveloped in the red mesh, we immediately saw the light being disassembled and it disappeared. I promised God right there that neither of us would ever attempt to photograph another of those sacred lights. We would begin understanding the next night, that the beautiful crystal lights were the finished product of the human spirit and soul. If they are not totally acceptable for heaven after death, they must be refined and educated during the millennium that will begin directly after Jesus returns back on earth. After more teaching along those lines several nights in that week, J and I would both start to understand that hell doesn't yet exist until the end of the thousand year reign of Jesus Christ. We would also learn there are really two holding areas beginning right after death, and they are separated by a divide that cannot be crossed by the ones held on the left side of that divide. That left side is where you go upon death if you are not right with God, but that is not Hell. The thousand year period allows for educating of those on the wrong side, so that they do not end up in Hell which is created at the end of the Millennium. That night as we went back in and sat down, we were allowed to actually see for the first time who had been erecting the lights. It was the older members of the B family from a week earlier. It confirmed what we thought earlier, that they really were saints and they were doing God's work on earth and in heaven. After that we decided to call it a night and we locked up the store together and left at the same time. J had only been working with me for one full week as of that evening, yet she had seen so many experiences with me. We had truly developed a good understanding with each other and I was really enjoying the experiences with her. I was married still but my marriage was only a shell of what I once had, and at a time that I truly needed someone to share beautiful things with. We were a lot of years apart, but we had both been put into a world of experiences that you couldn't talk to everyone about. I would later often talk to J about everything that we were encountering and how she handled it with others. She would say that she usually didn't tell anyone except her close childhood friend. J would always say that her friend knew that she was telling her the truth about it; even though J's father had recently said it wasn't really happening. That was the same man who had not believed the evidence of spirits in her life as a child. Little did J or I know but my wife had contacted J's father and told him that J and I must be hallucinating on some kind of drug, because the stories were too wild. That may have explained why her dad bought into my wife's story, but it was wrong both times. That shocked and further disappointed me with my wife that she was that desperate enough to try to discredit me in any way that she could. It was at that point that I very secretly began my own investigation into why she was doing all this to me. What I discovered was pretty shocking and a total surprise. My wife had enrolled in a program sponsored by a supposedly Christian church nearby under the auspices of the church minister, and that program was called by the unbelievable title a Pre-Divorce Class and it had begun in early 2011. It was in full swing at the time of the Joplin Tornado, and that would explain a lot of things that would continue to unfold. However, it would all become even clearer to me over the next two to three years. My wife had gone to that so called minister right after I told her about the woman who I seriously referred to as the *angel appearing on June 25, 2011.* The minister had told my wife that anyone who made such a statement of the things I was telling her of; would have to be suffering from a psychotic disorder, drugs, alcoholic delusions, or just be a plain liar. I was sorry to hear that the minister and his church were of the Methodist faith, because I was raised in a very different type of Methodist Church. The night of July 18, 2011 as I drove home, I tried for the thousandth time to make sense of what I was going through with my wife. I already knew there had to be an underlying reason for my wife to be trying to destroy my reputation as an honest person. Honesty was the most important attribute that I learned from both of my parents.

As usual I drove home in a somber mood, never knowing what I would encounter when I got there. It seemed to go from bad to worse and I enjoyed coming home less every time another event happened. It always would end up that I would be accused of being crazy about anything that I mentioned to her. Therefore, we had less to talk about, because the remarkable events at work were the only thing on my mind every waking moment. Most people cannot imagine the pain of having such an awesome gift from God, and then not being able to share it with family members. Another factor which added to that distress was that I would have never dreamed of God giving me such gifts anyway. Ironically, I was still generating every dollar that was brought into my family, yet I was accused of being insane. One thing for sure the gifts were going to increase in spiritual value, but my treatment at home would become worse. On June 25th the *angel* had said that God was about to bestow a very special gift upon me. She also said that no matter how bad it gets, He will never forsake you. In reality God would begin bestowing so many special gifts upon me, that it would become a most indescribable feeling that I really wanted my family to be able to appreciate it. Once I began fully knowing when God was responding to me, even the quietest reply that I knew came from Him, would be a most wonderful feeling.

As things got worse at home, I found myself calling on God almost every night could get some guidance from Him on things that were happening. God began speaking to me mostly through strong unmistakable feelings when I pondered questions to Him. He would often give me answers but some of the answers would be painful to this day, yet they were always correct. If He had an answer that was not going to be pleasing to me, I would ask him up to three times and he would finally answer me after the third time. I was seeing how God would sometimes answer me in a way which clearly demonstrated to me how sensitive He is to our emotions. I recall one instance where I asked God two times an emotionally painful question and got no answer, and the third time I asked He quietly said "probably not, " and I felt that His answer was no, but He just didn't want to say no, so He said probably not. He truly understood that His answer was painful and He didn't want to see me hurt. Tuesday July19, I went in at 4 in the afternoon and planned to stay overnight at the store. J was coming in at 4:30 and work until as long as she was needed. There would be times when God would want me alone to encounter a specific situation, and on those nights everything would be quiet until J left. Also there would be instances when J would be off for the night, and an event would happen with only me there after closing. That evening, we both expected to see a continuance of the prior night's activities. J and I worked on completing the lingerie inventory tagging and restocking the racks. We had pretty steady sales up until closing at midnight, and as we were locking the front door we noticed some of the young men in the colored outfits appearing. They had been only seen once every two or three days and then not for long. They were coming from the west parking lot toward the front of the store, as they always had previously. The young men had unfriendly and potentially evil outward appearance as they walked stiffly around the front area. Each one had their hair cut very short and they all looked possibly to have prison haircuts. Every time in the last month that we had encountered any of them, they were troublesome. As it was, these men were going to be representative of evil on this earth and choose not to believe in God. We would see that unless the elect (the saints) could change their beliefs, they would all be thrown into the Lake of Fire which is really The Consuming Fire of God. Their demeanor produced an outward appearance that depicted them as evil, with an agenda that they didn't want to be free of. I would eventually understand that the colors of their clothing represented the level of sin they were living with. The evil ones, after reappearing for more than an hour had then moved back into the far west parking area and then disappeared. We assumed that they were brought back to remind us that they were still part of the entirety of what we going to be shown. As soon as all of the evil appearing ones had gone, one of the beautiful crystal lights began forming adjacent to a large tree in the east corner of the property. The saints weren't visible but we knew that they were the ones who were building that light. The beautiful crystal was completed and it was being photographed in full range of the east outside corner camera. It would always be so disappointing that the store cameras would pick up these things but would not record them. Our personal cameras would take certain pictures and then they would instantly become covered with the red mesh. The store cameras would hold the same picture on the monitor as long as there was movement, the image would then disappear without any record. It was so unbelievably beautiful but we knew it would be gone at any time. We got up and went outside to within 20 feet of the light and we leaned against J's car. Suddenly at that instant the light exploded into a brilliant white powder form and an orb of super white light shot up over the building. The streaking light appeared to take an almost straight up course, and then instantly went out of sight. We walked around outside for a while and we were openly wondering what we had just seen. J and I I sat around a long while before calling it another very good night. We walked out to J's car with her and then stayed in the parking lot with Sheba for a few minutes. That morning it was probably 4AM before I got to sleep, but I slept well even if it was only 3 hours. The sheer adrenaline from everything going on in my life was keeping me going, and it would be that way for a very long time. I called C that morning and told her to come in Thursday morning, and that I was going to work both shifts on Wednesday. I had seen enough of the night events to know that these were going to continue for at least another night or two. J was to be back in by 4 that afternoon to work until whatever time things ended. While I was outside with Sheba that morning, I suddenly remembered that several things had been answered while I was sleeping. I knew then that the crystal lights were the perfected spirit and souls going back to the

Father from the hands of the saints. I also was made to understand that the lights which we had been seeing for the last two nights were of the good people who had been in my building since shortly after the tornado. It also occurred to me at that instant, of what the old minister had told me that afternoon in June as his son was changing my tire. He had said; "Son those poor souls are searching for the way home, and they will all leave before long." I understood that those souls were now going home and one day their relatives and friends would join them. I knew then that the well perceived old minister had been correct in probably everything that he had told me. That morning, I definitely knew that God really had sent him to me that afternoon. J got in that day at 3 instead of 4, and suggested that I take a nap for a couple of hours. I knew that she could handle the counter and would wake me if she needed help. The opportunity for me to catch a nap occasionally during the day would be something that I would begin to appreciate. It had been almost two months since the tornado, and my sleep had been scarce at best. Fortunately I didn't know it then, but my loss of sleep would become the norm for several years.

J had a pretty slow afternoon, but I got about two hours rest and felt pretty good. J went up to the pizza place and got dinner for us. Pizza was not my favorite food but it had been a while since we had one, anyway pizza happened to be Sheba's favorite people food. That Wednesday evening the store got pretty busy and the time passed by quickly. The last couple in the store that night went out ahead of me, and I locked the doors. I saw a light being erected on J's car which was parked a little to the east of the front door. There were constantly people on the cameras inside the store as if they were shopping, but many of them were just the friendly spirits who stayed there. It became something that fooled me quite often whenever I may take my eyes off the monitors. If I were to happen to go in the back office and look at the monitor again, I many times had to come out of the office to see if it was an actual customer. Every now and then early in the morning, there would be an older man who would come walking right up to the counter. Maybe it was a joke to them, but I was fooled by him a time or two, and I would ask him if I could help him. He would then quickly wheel around and go through the front inside wood door. There was a young blond haired lady in a red dress, which had been appearing in the store nightly right after we closed. She was in spirit form and had been appearing over the last several nights' right after closing. The majority of the spirits had become so common that unless we playfully sat down to watch their games, we just ignored their presence. That attractive mysterious lady in red as we began calling her, had nightly appeared nightly in almost the center of the lingerie area. She would be pulling out a particular colored dress and pushing it back over and over again. We never were able to see her face from where she was standing, and she never turned around facing any camera. J was constantly wishing out loud that we could see her face and possibly identify her from the pictures. There would come a time that would to be J's last night working on September 26, 2011 that J would say; "it has been four months since the tornado and she is still here. The young lady instantly turned around and looked directly at us, and she then disappeared forever from the store. The light that had formed out front on J's car stayed there for more than an hour, before it exploded into a bright white powder. Then instantly another white ball of light shot into the sky just as the one the night before. That same process would be seen once every several nights, and J and I were witness to it happening maybe 15 times over the next month. Occasionally after closing, we would see a super white light somewhere around the property. We saw a light one night that was all the way back to the creek that was adjacent to the Trail of Tears crossing site. We were also noticing that there was a slight decline in the number of the men, women and children in the store. Originally there must have been close to 25 of the good seeming entities with us there in the building area, now there seemed to be maybe 20. It hadn't quite occurred to us yet, but the friendly entities who had appeared in the store after the tornado, were the ones that we were actually seeing being processed back to the Father. I had recently noticed something unusual on the recorded camera logs that appeared as a foggy area near the west corner of my business property. That location was between the store and I-44 actually within 60-70 yards of the interstate, but still appearing as on my property. It was only showing during clear nights and usually way after midnight. I didn't mention it to anyone yet but I started doing some research into it. That foggy looking area on the edge of my property would turn out to be a very "special gift" from God. That gift would explain so many incidents that had been taking place daily for almost two months, and we never realized it. The spiritual phenomena would prove to also become a conduit back and forth from Satan. I would soon learn that a dimensional portal had been opened since just after the Joplin tornado. The portal had opened below the route of The Trail of Tears, which the Cherokee People called "The Trail Where They Cried."That Portal existence would force me to develop a faith in God, which was going to carry me through hundreds of nightmarish encounters. Albert Einstein had a theory about Portals that they allowed good into and out of our world, but they had the same purposes for evil. That area that all of the beautiful light orbs had been projected into had been the portal. It would be several weeks before I would be enlightened to what a Portal was and who was using it for sinister purposes. The sinister purposes would expose a most evil enemy who would eventually cause me to intentionally close my business there. Things had begun making more sense slowly, but the discernment from God was going to be an ongoing gift and many more things would be disclosed to me over time.

J and I both were going home that night after several hours but were both planning to be in by 5PM the next day, which was Thursday July 21st. That night I was driving drive home in my compact car with Sheba. My nightly habit was to constantly view the outside vehicles for entities, before I started out to the car. That night when I looked at my car on the monitor, it was full of the evil ones as we had begun calling the young men in the colored outfits. In addition to that, J had at least one of the same ones in her car as well. Just as we started out to leave we were looking at her car on the cameras, and something suddenly appeared on the inside of the windshield. We went out the door and locked up all the doors at that time. J's car was parked several spaces away from my truck, so I walked over to her car to look inside at what was on her windshield. As she unlocked the door, she said there is an awful sickening smell in here. I stuck my head inside and it was a nauseating odor like I had never smelled. I would describe the odor as like some sort of intense smelling dry-cleaning fluid, and it made you literally want to throw up. That same nauseating smell would later become so common, that it would nightly make Sheba sick enough that she would throw up. Then J said whatever that is on the windshield looks like mud and it is still wet. It was a blob like smear, which we were never able to understand its origin except that it was put there by one of the paranormal evil ones. That smell would become synonymous with obvious devilish entities that were suddenly now in our presence. J sat down in her car and cranked it, and then she screamed at me to look at her purse which was on the seat beside her. She had a rather large white leather mesh purse and it was open at the top. Absolutely everything in it was being scooped out into the seat, and you couldn't see anything that was scooping it out. She was quickly putting things back in it, but they were being shoveled back out. I had never seen anything like it before, but we would see much worse things in the future. That episode quieted down but all the way home she kept calling me and saying that whatever it was, it was still in her car. I had stayed behind J until she turned off in Joplin to get to her house, just in case something else happened. She got home alright, but the next day she told me that the little mischievous ghost had gone through her kitchen cabinets at her house. The next morning things were all over the counter and kitchen floor, in addition to her lamp being turned on and off all night even after she unplugged it. She would also tell me the next day that the little bugger had came back to the store with her.

The next day was Thursday the 21st of July, and J and I both got in at 5 in the afternoon. We were both wondering what was on tap for the night, considering how things had turned nasty the night before. She got involved with several different lingerie customers while I was busy at the front desk. The afternoon and evening had gone by and neither of us had eaten. Then close to 11:30 I watched on the cameras as another beautiful light was going up next to the east fence, just about halfway between the building and I-44. This time it looked like a good sized group of people maybe 12 or so, was within close proximity to the light. We could definitely recognize the three B sons and the two older men, as well as some other men who had been in the rear of the meeting group nearly two weeks earlier. Just like a couple of nights earlier, the B men were all dressed in sparkling white linen looking shirts and trousers. I had been made to understand that the white linen material outfits were identifying them as Saints, and were some of God's chosen ones. As had always happened in each learning event, store business was done for the night when the spirits appeared. We had learned that when the event started before normal closing time, it was because no more customers were coming anyway. That night we went ahead and locked up the doors to wait for the production to begin. As soon as we had the doors all locked, we saw exactly 12 people standing conspicuously in the cameras view. It was so enjoyable each night that we looked forward to it, never knowing what we would witness. At that moment there was the brilliant white explosion powder, but that time as the white ball of light shot upward there was a loud explosion for our attention. It was all produced that way in order to drive home to us what exactly was taking place. As quickly as that had happened, we saw 5 groups of two men each in the white linen clothing walking away from where the light had been. There was an area in the very front of my store on both sides of the front door entrance, which was all grass. Most always that area was where I parked whatever vehicle I was driving that day. That particular night I was in my Black Hyundai and it was pulled in parallel to the store, which made it clearly visible on three main outside store cams. I went to the soft drink machine which was in the front foyer just inside the door. J yelled at me to look through the glass door at what was next to my car. I looked out to the right and within 10 feet of the store building; there was a pit that was filled with literally boiling red and blue liquids that were obviously producing volcanic like heat. Smoke was slowly swirling around my car which was on the outside edge of the fire. That way it was not seen from the interstate even if one could see the supernatural images. Even with all the things that we had witnessed, it was still hard to believe that we were seeing yet this awesome event right next to us. I walked back to the counter and sat down, and J asked me what we were seeing. I had already determined that it was the 'fire and brimstone" of Hell, but didn't know why we were seeing it there. Just as I answered her question as to what it was, there appeared the 10 men in white moving toward the fire. Each pair of the "saints" had one of the tall evil ones in the colored outfits walking between them and being held by each arm; it was obvious that they were going to put them into the "fire and brimstone." The 5 evil entities were each dressed in one of the red outfits and accompanying one of them was a large black vicious looking dog. The 10 "saints" brought the men and the large dog forward and they stopped directly between my car and the edge of the boiling lava-like fire. Then ever so bizarre as we watched intently, the first evil one in line fully in sight of us instantly tore an arm loose from his guard and leaned over to my right rear car window. He quickly drew or wrote something on the dust and dew-covered car window. Then that man, along with the other 4 young men were each raised up by their armpits and pitched into the swirling blue and red lava, along with the big black dog. After that was completed, immediately every one of the saints disappeared back to the east side of the building. Everything had been so realistic and pointed, that J and I were just sitting and staring at each other saying nothing. As we watched the fire disappear over the next few minutes, it was obvious that we were each deep in our own thoughts about what we had seen. That had been the most gut-wrenching performance yet, and I could feel a definite intent for not ending up in that same fire. Whenever we did begin talking about what we had just witnessed, it was evident we both were touched personally by it. The weightiest feeling was the awesomeness of knowing for a fact, that God Himself had just produced and directed that entire production for the two of us. I tried to stress to J that all these events were definitely direct messages from God, and I reminded her of everything that the *angel* had said to me nearly a month ago. J agreed that God definitely intended for us to tell other people of the things that we were being shown. Although as always, she would tell me that most people were never going to believe her, even though she knew how real it all was. I would always try to reassure her, that God Himself was giving us these gifts and they were to be shared with others. We had forgotten all about seeing the young man scribble something on my car window that morning. J promised to be back that afternoon before 6, and I walked out to her car with her. After she left I had to go back inside to turn out the lights before I could leave. When Sheba and I started to leave I noticed there was not one entity in my car that night. It was so awesome to think that all the spirits around my building had also watched that production, and they certainly knew how real it was. Then when I let Sheba jump into the car on the passenger side, I remembered seeing the young man drawing something on my car window. I shut the door and turned around and there on my right back window, he had quickly drawn a Swastika as his last action before being tossed into the fire of Hell. As I drove the 52 miles home to Oklahoma, just as we had felt earlier, I again was in a rather pensive mood. By the time I got home and finally was able to get to sleep, it was already getting daylight. I had only gotten maybe four hours sleep before I decided to get up and get going, since I had a couple of things to do before I went to work.

I knew that one of the most difficult things for J to understand was why God would choose us to teach these lessons to. I had that very same question to begin with, but a while after the *angel* had been and delivered the beautiful message on June 25, I knew that it was all truly happening for a reason. I also well remembered the questions that were in my mind about why me, and how the *angel* had even known my questions before I could ask them. Her very first answer to my first thought of; I am not deserving of God bestowing special gifts upon me, was that "God sees the good in you; He doesn't see the bad." I told J one day that I never awoke in the morning, when I didn't have a hard time realizing that all those things were happening to me. Today twelve years later, I still feel the same way and I know that I am the luckiest man in the world even on my worst days. Even after all those times and so many beautiful experiences since, I still battle with the devil and his cohorts every day and night. I wasn't sinless then and neither will I be the day I leave this flesh body. My lesson from God was that He will accept us all as sinners, and He will help us to lessen our degree of sin while He is teaching us faith. Additionally, God will forgive us of all our sins as Jesus promised; seven times seventy and that all we need to do is to ask. God's intervention in my life in my 65th year proved without a doubt, that one does not have to be even close to good. It showed me that God will accept anyone that He has chosen, and He will mold that one into a new person. The difference with me was that I absolutely had no choice but to be molded, and God reminded me in unique ways that I well understood. However, He gave me such awesome gifts of discernment and beauty that I wanted to become a better person. Simply put though, no one can ever be perfect as long as they are in the flesh body on this earth, because Jesus was the only perfect one that ever walked this earth. Even with all the glorious feelings that I was appreciating, I was hurt badly from the fact that my family couldn't see and appreciate the unbelievable gift that we had been given. That gift was intended as a blessing for the entire family, and all they had to do was trust me as they always had. For J, A, a number of other employees and close associates, it is my hope that you will always remember those miraculous things that you witnessed from God. As of those times, I want to again remind you as I always did then, that those supernatural events were not brought about by me, but were only from God. There were times when employees and friends, had told me how they had never seen things, like those that they witnessed while working with me. I always made it a point then to explain to each of them, that the spiritually beautiful events had always come from God. I know that as God began working in my life in 2011, 2012 and 2013, He purposely allowed certain other people in my life to see miracles that most had never witnessed. At times when I had prayed to God for help in their presence, I would always remind them that the answer to that prayer would come from Him, not from me. I had several times told them to tell their children, grandchildren and all who would listen, about the wonderful things that God had done in their presence. I know for a fact, that He purposely gives us miraculous evidence of His Existence in our lives, and that He really wants us to share that undeniable proof with others. That is precisely why this true story was written about The Battle of Good and Evil, which is a battle that is quickly concluding in this earth age.

That afternoon it was well before 5 when I got to work, but I let C go ahead and leave. It was Friday July 22, and it had been another awesome week for us each night. I found myself as I did every day, wondering what was to come. However, had I known of all that was to come, I don't know if I would have been able to handle it. J got in at 6 and went to work on restocking some inventory with me. As the afternoon turned to evening, it became busy like most Friday evenings in the summer. I had loaned a woman some money on an older ATV, which she had brought in to me to hold until she paid me back. She was related to a woman who used to work for me, and I figured that she would eventually pay me back. As it was, she said she only needed the money for two weeks, so I never even took the ATV off my truck. It was worth more than I had loaned her, but it needed a new battery in it to crank it. I had taken the old battery out to put a new one in that she had purchased, but I just had not installed it. The business got really slow so we decided to close early at 11:45. Then right after I locked the side doors, I looked out onto the northeast side of the property, and I saw some of the B family men in the rear part of the pasture. They all looked so alive and appeared as if they were in flesh bodies, yet they obviously were all in spiritual bodies. It was the original five men who had been at our meeting two weeks earlier, and they were also part of the group from the night before. They were all dressed in the sparkling white linen clothing just as the night before. I called J and showed them to her even though they were probably 200 yards away, because I knew there was more action to come that night. We went back inside and turned off the rest of the outside lights, got two soft drinks out and sat down behind the counter. Then right away we saw that there was another fire and brimstone pit starting to boil up. That afternoon before I got to work, a trucker had a mechanical problem with his truck and C had let him park it overnight between the store and the highway. The fire was in a location this time closer to the front entrance and the interstate, and we knew that anyone who could see spirits would certainly see it, if not for that semi which was blocking the view. I was surprised that the fire was actually appearing so close to I-44, but I wouldn't have had any decision in it if I could have. That evening began with a horde of the young men dressed exactly as the others, and they were again coming from the back of the west parking area. The five men and another who had now joined them were escorting three young men in colored outfits toward the fire. Those three men were brought straight across my front parking area to the rolling fire, and pitched in one at a time by two men who held them. Within another half hour the scene was repeated with three more of the apparent unbelievers. This went on for three times that night, with nine more young men being pitched into the consuming fire before the fire went out. As we usually did after the events, we sat inside and talked about what we had seen that night. It was apparent to us that God was now showing us that the evil ones were part of the group that had been in my building since the start. The prayers to keep the evil out of the midst of the good ones had worked pretty well, but I couldn't take any credit for that. It had gotten to the point that I tried have two meetings weekly with the good spirits who were inside the building. Also whenever I had problems inside from the evil, I could call for the "all my good people" to actually help me get rid of the bad ones inside. They would all fan out in whichever section of the building that I told them and would actually force the evil ones out. Sometimes they would battle physically for as long as thirty minutes, and I can never to this day understand how they were doing it. There would be things falling off shelves and racks, and I could always immediately see the difference after they did that for me. It was another of the beautiful things that I gained from those friendly and very real spirits who would reside in my store for two months. I was having interactions with them, which it seemed no one had ever heard of anything similar. I knew that I was going to miss them when they were gone. I could tell that there were several leaving every week, and that was exactly what the old pastor had promised me would happen. He had told me that those poor souls were looking for the way home. They knew that it was exactly what was intended for them, and it was certainly what they looked forward to. It was no doubt that it was God's plan to teach us the truth that all must be taught, before it is too late. We were also two of those that were learning at that time as well, because it all was making a lasting impression.

I had been constantly wondering how long it would be before I would full understand everything that was taking place in my life. I knew that it was about me changing my life, but I still hadn't determined what it was that the *angel* had meant that God needed me to do. It wasn't going to be too much longer before events would begin giving me a lot of understanding. Once it began it was going to be a very long-term project to completion. On the brighter side, most everything that we had been exposed to daily and nightly had been friendly for the most part. Yet I knew that there had to be something much bigger still waiting out there, that I was going to personally have to deal with. We had began seeing a darker side of that spirit world, but we just didn't realize how much darker it was going to get. I was going to finally learn that I had been enrolled in God's Crash Course on Spirits, as I would begin calling it. My last two months had only been basic training for the real trials that were going to start on August 6, 2011. That battle would be against enemies, who were more evil and supernaturally powerful than anyone could ever have imagined. Some would be from other worlds and some would be from earth, but they would all have the same evil leader.

It was something after 3AM and J and I were both going to be leaving at about the same time. J drove off maybe five minutes behind J, after I let Sheba run around a bit in the front lot. Then as I cranked my truck, J called me telling me that something was again in her car. Her car lights were being turned off as she drove along I-44, and as she pulled over, they would come back on. We both knew what it was; it was the nasty ones doing their usual evil. This was constantly happening to her, so I told her to pull off past the Kansas City Exit and wait for me. Whenever I got to where J was stopped, I told her to pull out ahead of me and I would stay behind her until we got to Joplin. At that point I suppose the evil one moved into my truck, because things got really crazy. I still had the ATV in the back of my truck and it still had no battery in it. Suddenly, as J was safely able to go onto her house, I turned onto the Highway 71 South Exit toward Oklahoma. I got into traffic with several semis all going south at 4AM on Saturday morning. Then I heard air horns blowing at me from behind, and they were blinking their lights as well. I looked in my outside mirrors and saw what they were blowing at. The rear tail lights on the ATV in my truck had come and they were blinking on and off. I knew that wasn't possible since there was no battery in it, then it hit me. The evil one was playing with J's lights had now started with the ATV lights. I pulled over beside the road and got out, and the lights went off. When I got back in my truck and started off they came on again, and that time even the headlight on the ATV was on. Sheba was in the back seat and the light was blinding her as she tried to see what was happening. As I was driving about 70 miles per hour, the headlight turned off and stretched across my back truck window, it was a very large white ghost that looked like Casper. He had each arm stretched from one side of my back sliding window to the other. He was holding on tight, and it looked like his mouth was a suction cup locked onto the top center of my back window. Trucks were honking their horns and blinking their lights frantically. I will never forget, there was two big electric company bucket trucks and another semi with two power poles on it all travelling together. They had probably been one of the many electric companies volunteering to put Joplin utilities back together from the May tornado. They each had Arkansas tags and had probably worked all night and were going home for some rest. There were several men in each of the three trucks, and they did not believe what they were seeing in my truck. They all followed me until I got off Highway 71 not too far from Arkansas. I always imagined how they probably have never stopped talking about what they saw that morning, and how so many people have called them crazy. That ghost hung on my rear glass window until I drove up to my farm gate that morning. It was just starting to get daybreak, as the big white mischievous ghost disappeared around my barn. Those overnight ghost pranks will be more of those weird, but true events that I will always remember. It really wasn't mean, but it did prove without a doubt that ghosts do have a sense of humor. I would have loved to have had someone who would have appreciated hearing that story that morning, but instead I went into my house and went right to sleep. I had been up for a long 24 hours, and I had to go back that afternoon. The next day was Saturday July 23, and J and I were both going to be at work by 5 in the afternoon. Saturday after we got in and got organized, it started out like it was going to be a slow evening. Since we had a shipment of items that had been only partly catalogued, we both began working on finishing that up. As it turned out, business got pretty brisk from 7 until 10 and then it totally dried up. I decided even though it was Saturday night, we may close an hour early if business didn't pick up. It was just as we started to close right before 11PM, that I saw one of the beautiful crystal lights being erected on J's car, which was parked just one space east of the front door. It was pretty obvious that it was supposed to get our full attention. We left the doors unlocked and outside lights on, even though no one had ever driven up when something was taking place in the parking lot. Just as were sitting behind the counter watching the monitors, a new looking pickup came driving in to the front of the store. It was an older couple and they parked exactly two spaces to the west side of the door. They came in and it was a couple from Springfield that we had never seen before. She was a retired registered nurse who was apparently a Christian. As J was talking to her, the woman asked if she could sit in one of several chairs in the lobby. She had an old knee injury and was talking about that with us, as her husband quietly listened. I was behind the counter, and saw that the light was being taken down off J's car. Next thing we saw, it was now going up in the middle of the sidewalk coming from the center of the parking area. The woman overheard us talking about the light and wanted to see it, so I let her come around and look at it on the monitors. We told her about things we had been witnessing for two months, and she truly believed us. She showed the light to her husband and I heard him whisper that it had to be some kind of faulty camera problem. At that point the light was then taken down from off the sidewalk, and it was going up right outside my front entrance next to the door. The lights were exactly as the spirits had always been; they could be seen by J and me because we were able to also see spirits. Anyone could see it all happening on the surveillance monitors, but no one could record them or take a picture of them. Instead of the crystal light being put directly in the middle of the door way entrance; it was put slightly to the right outside edge for a specific reason that we didn't yet know. Only God could have known to put that light on that side of the door entrance, because it was precisely where Sheba and I were going to walk. When they both saw the light through the door and on the monitor, the husband told his wife that they needed to leave. At ten minutes until midnight, the woman told her husband that he knew that it was God's Work, but he was just uncomfortable with anything about God. She told us that she had better go with him and she was very sorry about his actions. I was kind of glad to see him leaving, so I held her arm and walked her out to their car. I got on her right side to go out the front door, and that put me in line with the crystal light. I was paying close attention to her walking on my left side, since she was having such a hard time with her knee. Just as we walked out the door, I realized that I had stepped right into the shimmering crystal light as if it wasn't there. J screamed at the top of her lungs as she came running out the door to get me. As I was helping the elderly woman in their car and saying good night, J was excitedly telling to me what had happened. As I walked through that beautiful light, it had instantly become engulfed in a beautiful thick scarlet colored smoke slowly swirling around me. I could clearly see the scarlet smoke slowly rising as I turned and started back inside. We sat back down behind the counter and were talking and watching the monitors and the phone rang. I answered it and it was my wife, and I could see that it was only three minutes until midnight. Suddenly there was a man who could have been me, and he was rising up slowly out of the scarlet smoke. Ironically he was dressed in one of the former evil group's outfits, and it was a light scarlet colored pants and shirt. He was rising so very slowly with his head and hands held up like in a praying position high above his head, and he was looking upward. My wife began asking me how things were going, and I was hurriedly trying to explain what was happening before our eyes at that very moment. As I was on the phone with her still, the man was standing fully upright reaching his hands high up in a most humble prayer position. Then suddenly there was an explosion louder than a firecracker, the man went straight up and out of sight over the building, just as the white light orbs had done for weeks. My wife couldn't or wouldn't be able to understand any part of the described performance, but she hadn't witnessed it either. J and I talked about that happening for a long time that night and for days afterward. We had both assumed that God was showing us that even bad ones can change enough to be acceptable by Him. It has now been several years since that night July 23, 2011, when only a few minutes were left before midnight. God has bestowed so many spiritually powerful gifts upon me since that night 12 years ago. Yet only recently, have I realized that the man in the scarlet outfit with the scarlet smoke swirling around him, most likely represented all. God was showing us that it is almost midnight in our lives, and that we are very close to the Seventh and final Trump of Revelations. In a slow astonishing discovery over the years, I realized that in the summer of 2011, J and I had literally been part of real live productions that were directly from God. I had finally understood that many different events were taking me to Revelations, the Final Chapter of the Bible. Beginning that August 6, the real tests and teachings were going to take me deep into Revelations and the End Times Prophesies of the Bible. J and I had been through the easy part, while I was being prepared for the toughest battles of my life. J would be leaving in late

September and I would face the toughest enemies after she left. I am convinced that God place J in my life on July 11 for a distinct purpose, and it began on her first night there. She definitely helped me during some most unusual times and I will always remember her for those times.

I knew that we had been given the luxury of witnessing things in both flesh and spiritual bodies. Over the next nearly two weeks J and I worked nights, except J didn't work Sundays. The nightly events were pretty much quieting down except for some fire and brimstone events on two more nights. It seemed that almost all of the evil ones within the group had just about received their just rewards. Things were getting so much quieter even on the outside of the building at night. I called "all my friends" in the store together that evening. I had begun getting them together once or twice a week for the last two weeks, since I realized that they were all slowly leaving. J was off that evening with her children, but an associate of mine came in the store after 9 that night. He was sitting behind the counter with me, and I told him that I was having a meeting in a few minutes with the entities in the store. T was not sure if they would appear with him sitting there, but I knew that they would be there if he was not uncomfortable. I explained that to him, and he thought it was really awesome that he would be able to sit there around them. Then he wanted to know if he could call his wife to come over to join us. I decided that from what he told me, his wife would not be real comfortable so I told him no. I had told "my spirit friends" that afternoon that the meeting would be between 9 and 10, and I always would walk into the back room to call them. They would all then start appearing around the counter from different directions, and Sheba would always personally greet each one of them. Sheba seemed to especially adore them and they loved her as well, and it was so beautiful to watch them hugging on her. It was hard to imagine that were only a total of seven of them still left in the building, considering how many had been there originally. I had been sensing for several days that something was bothering them, and I had tried very hard to understand what it was. They could understand me perfectly but I couldn't now understand them, except that they were very fearful of something. They were in a different dimension so their speech sounded very fast, to the level that you couldn't decipher it. Their voices had never been clear to me from the start, as some of the B family had been, but I had always been able to perceive most of their thoughts. I could clearly sense that it was a pending fear of something or someone. I knew that they were excited about them all leaving for a special place, so I knew their fear or dread had to be of something else. That night, I tried really hard to find a way to understand what it was that they were worrying about. I even tried asking questions about different things which they could just answer yes or no to, but that seemed to frustrate them even more so I stopped. It had been like that for the last two meetings that we had, and I would always feel so bad that I wasn't able to understand them in our last meeting. They would be gone by the time I would realize that their worries were not about themselves, but were about me. Once we die here and become instantly changed into a spirit body, we then have 100% recall of literally everything that ever transpired in our lives. Even more awesome, in the spiritual body one can see things that are going to happen in both the spirit world and the flesh world. My "good friends" could see that a most evil and powerful enemy was about to appear in my world, and they wanted so badly to tell me who it was. Even more amazing, was that they knew that this would be the battle that God had been preparing me for, and they wanted so badly to tell me that. I had thought for a week that it was something that they were fearful of for themselves, but instead they were anxious for me to know who it was that was coming. That was how close I came to understanding their very last messages. I know now, that they knew that I would make it through the really bad times with the help of God, but I believe they just wanted show their caring for me. I had early on learned that good spirits only want to be accepted by those of us still in flesh bodies, and I had been taught by God how to accept them. That Friday night they also knew that they would all be leaving for an even better world in two days. I noticed that after my friend had left that night around 11, my spirit friends kept staying around in the office. I had a couple of customers that were in the store and they both left around 11:30. Then after the two customers left, "my remaining friends" came out of the back office. They were all lounging on the floor behind the counter playing with Sheba, but they were definitely watching me. It was not the way they usually were, because they never had just stayed that long around me as they did that night. Within a couple of days I would know that they had all been saying goodbye. When Sheba and I locked up after midnight, the three women and four men were standing in the foyer as we left. Being friendly, I asked if anyone wanted to go to Grand Lake with us, just like I used to always ask when I was going to Oklahoma. I knew they wouldn't go, because they had stopped going with me several weeks ago when the nightly events began. They looked happy with my offer but kind of nodded their heads not. As I put Sheba in the car, I could see them still standing inside the door watching for us to drive off. While driving to Oklahoma, I was assuming that they would still be there the next afternoon when I got in, and was also planning that J would see them again also before they left. She and I were going to be in at 3 the next day, but that would become a day that would become another landmark event date. I had many unbelievable and pleasant memories of the last two months, experiences that could not be described by any single word or phrase that I could think of. I had a difficult time understanding how I had been able to have all the interactions with those different spiritual bodies. Since I knew that it was not anything that anyone I talked to had ever heard of, it could have only been one of the blessings that had come from God. It had to be another gift from Him, but it was only a drop in the bucket compared to all the beautiful gifts that He was going to give me.

That night as I drove home to Oklahoma, I had so many different emotions. I had been stressed so much over the last two months that I rarely felt totally rested, and I was really needing a good night's rest. If I could get a good night's sleep it would be a blessing because I was feeling quite worn out.

The next morning when I awoke, I realized how tired I had been because it was 11am. I overslept by not setting my clock, but that several hours of extra sleep was going to be a blessing. I was planning to be in to work by 4:30 that afternoon, but I needed to leave in time to go through Joplin for something. As I drove away from the farm that afternoon, little did I know but that day Saturday August 6, 2011, would forever be burned into my memory. I was 65 years old and I had been in some pretty rough situations, but this was going to be absolutely the toughest challenge of my life. For more than two months day and night I had lived in a world of spirits, and they were mostly friendly. Since June 25th, I had constantly wondered what the angel meant when she said, that God never told her "how bad it would be or how long it would last." I was about to know that this was the battle that God had been preparing me for, but I wouldn't know how long it would last either. However, I would learn how bad it would be real soon, because I would incur daily and nightly encounters with powerful supernatural enemies from other worlds.

When I got to the store it was a little after 4 that afternoon and there were several cars there. I usually parked on the grassy area just to the west side of the front door and very close the building. I let my employee leave at 4:30 as planned because J was to be in at 4:30 also. Then she called that she was going to be a little late, maybe it would be closer to 5. I knew that I may well need some help at the counter unless it slowed down some. I still had a good many people in the store when J got there at 5, so she helped me through the rush. Business had slowed somewhat by 5:45, so I went to work on a project that I had in my office to finish. There were several people who came in and were looking at merchandise around the store. I saw two different customers coming to the counter to check out merchandise, and I glanced at the wall clock. It was right at 6PM then, as J walked briskly into my office. Her quiet words were that I should look at my car on the outside cameras, because there was some "crazy looking stuff in it." I had driven my Hyundai, and it was parked within ten feet of two cameras and maybe within 25 feet of another. I adjusted the monitor and zoomed in on my car, and it appeared that there were four individuals in it, two in the front seat and two in the back. I could see that there was what appeared to be a very old white haired man in the front passenger seat. Then in the driver seat it looked like a late fortyish age man behind the steering wheel, and he had a large white bandage around the top part of his head. There were two individuals on each side of the rear seat who appeared to be juveniles. As I got up and walked by the counter I whispered to J to not say anything to the customers about this. I walked out the front door to my car and went up to the driver side. I tried to get the attention of the man with the bandage, but he looked like he was in a stupor and didn't even look at me. He looked dead but I knew that he was alive by his sitting with his hands on my steering wheel. I was within eighteen inches of him through the window and could see that the bandage was around the top crown of his head. Also there were real dark bloodstains around the very top of the bandage. The man had his hands on my steering wheel but he looked like he was in another world mentally. I walked around the front of the car and continued sizing up the situation. As I came around to the passenger side, it was obvious that the old man inside was not just old, but was very old and looked way more than one-hundred years old. I knew that I had never seen anyone that old before, and certainly not in my car. He appeared to be probably slightly over seven feet tall and was very thin, and his face was really gaunt almost like a skeleton face. He was looking quite stoically at me through the right front window of the locked door. I had the car keys, but I didn't really care at that point about the macabre passengers getting out and I sure didn't want to get in with them. Then as the old man unemotionally stared straight ahead, I was able to turn my attention to the disgusting reality of the two creatures in the back seat. As I was contemplating my next move, a couple who I had known for some time drove up and parked directly in front, and within ten feet of my car. The man started coming over to talk to me, but I quietly motioned to him that I would come inside with him shortly. The last thing that I needed was the news media being called in by someone right then. I shifted my attention back to the passenger side of the rear seat, where staring at me was the unusually small face of a possibly 12 year old boy. His green eyes were intently focused on my every move, and in total astonishment I realized that his entire body was that of a dark grey mottled snake, even including his head. I could see that the boy's small face was clearly only the very front part of the snake's elongated head. The snake-boy's thin arms came out of what would be the snake's shoulder area, and the arms which were no more than 12 inches long, had very small hands that were attached below each elbow. I could determine at that point that the rest of the snake like body was wrapped under him in the seat, and I saw no evidence of any legs. I didn't need to go back around to the other side of the car at that time, because I could see what was sitting on that side. It was another seemingly 12 year old with a tiny humanlike face and head, but it was obviously that of a small girl. The top of the little girl's head had light brown hair, which appeared to have been trimmed to right above the top of her very small ears. Then in even more disbelief, I realized that her body which started at the chin was really the body of the largest brown feathered duck that I had ever seen. Even crazier, the small amount of light brown hair was exactly the same shade of light brown as the duck's feathers. I could see that the duck's thick looking neck was connected directly below the chin and extended down 8-10 inches, and then connected into the very stout looking body. There were two very short arms of maybe 12 inches, with tiny hands that appeared to be smaller than the snake-boy's hands. The short arms came out from where a duck's wings would normally be attached to the body. Unlike the snake boy with apparently no legs, the duck girl had two short stubby legs which were each no more than 15 inches long. She had two exceptionally large duck- like webbed feet, that later would appear to be maybe 5-6 inches long as almost as wide. As I stood there gazing at those two in the back seat, and then at the zombie looking man holding onto my steering wheel, I felt nauseated. I remember thinking a thousand different things at that instant, but none of it made any sense to me. I was wondering where they came from and why were they all n my car, and most important what should I do. I remember one thing I was thinking, and that was that I didn't want to get in my car again. I had seen many so called freaks of nature shows in fairs and carnivals, but nothing could beat the grotesque bunch that had somehow gotten planted in my car. Then as I looked back at the old man in front, it was obvious that he wasn't concerned about what my reaction was, because he was only looking straight ahead at nothing. As crazy as it was, the seven feet tall string bean looking old man appeared to be the caretaker, for the entire ghoulish display that was my car. The one with the blood stained bandage around the primary motor cortex area of his head, truly appeared to us as a real zombie like we had watched in horror movies. I had watched him a good while and he had totally no reaction to anything, and was pretty pathetic looking hanging on to my steering wheel. Always one to try to turn lemons into lemonade, I thought I had a brilliant idea and nodded to the old man that I would be right back.

I walked inside and saw that there were no customers left in the store. I saw that J had been zoomed in on the main monitor and had been watching me outside. She had a good picture of everything that I had just been dealing with. When J had gotten to work at 5, I told her as soon as we got a break I would buy a pizza if she would go and pick it up. She wasn't laughing when she then asked if I still wanted to get a pizza and in the same breath asked;"what are they anyway?" I could tell she wasn't very hungry now either. I told her to come with me out to the car to see them up close, and she reluctantly followed me to the back of the car. She stopped and told me that she didn't really want to go up close, so I told her to look at the interior and two exterior mirrors. She couldn't see as clearly as going up to the car, so she finally agreed to look at them up close. As J approached the car on the passenger side, it suddenly appeared that the ancient old man had come back to life. It became quite obvious that the stoic old man from another world, really liked earth ladies because he wasn't stoic any longer. She gently elbowed me and whispered that he had; "kind of smiled at her," and then she turned and said "now I am really getting sick." I had to start laughing to try to preserve my sanity, so I started back inside the building and J was behind me saying; "you are not leaving me out here." We got inside the building and I told her about a great plan that I had. At that point, I was already correctly assuming that everything in my car, had come from somewhere other than our dimension. The old man looked possibly human, but yet his face was almost like a skeleton face at Halloween. He reminded me of a show that my children watched when they were very young, and a bad character in it was called Skeletor. I had been an accomplished connoisseur of Jack Daniels Whiskey throughout much of my earlier adult life. In my office was the last fifth of whiskey that I would ever own and it had been there almost a year. I had quit drinking all alcohol several years before, but a friend had given that bottle to me as a gift over the past Christmas. I told J that I thought we may secure a great financial windfall by offering the things in my car the Jack Daniels, in exchange for pictures of real life extra terrestrial beings. Then we could provide the pictures as evidence, along with the poster proposal to the Jack Daniels Distributors. The commercial could say that even aliens will smile for Jack Daniels Whiskey. I thought it was a great idea but I didn't know at that time, that it is not easy to get a clear picture of extra terrestrials. I would soon find out that they may smile, but they won't intentionally give you a picture. They would get the whiskey and J and I would take tons of pictures, but they would all be without any corresponding images. I told J since she had prettier printing than me, that I wanted her to make a sign for us. I had not asked the old man if he understood English, but I assumed stupidly that maybe he didn't. I was soon going to learn that all the other worlds know English, and no wonder they think we are dumb. Anyway I got out a sheet of white poster paper and J printed the following which I dictated; I will give you this bottle of whiskey, if you allow us to take as many pictures as we want to take tonight. I took the Jack Daniels and the poster out to the car for my offer to the old timer. I walked up to the front passenger window where the old man was, and in one hand I held up the whiskey and in the other hand held the poster. The skeleton looking face was very slightly smiling and he was slowly nodding his head yes. It wouldn't take long for me to realize that the very ancient old man had gotten the best end of that deal. That disappointing lesson learned on my first ever encounter with extra terrestrial beings, would be repeated probably many hundreds of times over the next two years. The lesson was that very rarely will an ET from any world allow a decent photo be taken of him. Occasionally there will only be a small area of grey paranormal fog in the picture, and at night the extra terrestrials will appear only as colored lights with sometimes a small amount of white and grey fog. I would discover eventually, that if you look very carefully in a picture of an extraterrestrial, you can usually detect a tiny bit of white or grey somewhere. I then took the bottle of whiskey and carefully set it on the far center edge of the front hood area. The old man knew exactly what we what we were thinking by strategically placing the bottle the way I had. We really wanted to see the duck girl or the snake boy go out and get the bottle, so J and I quickly went back inside to get behind the counter monitors. We had barely gotten to the counter and sat down at the monitors when it happened. Not one, but both of the young cloned creatures very slowly began moving toward the hood, and both were honestly slower than a small turtle, as they inched forward. All of my car windows were always up and the cars locked when parked at the store, but these entities were clearly paranormal and they didn't need keys or open windows. As J and I watched with baited breath, we were totally ecstatic at what we realized was literally happening in front of us. The duck girl and snake boy were still moving snail pace through the car toward the hood. They were staying precisely even and I mean precisely, with each other as they inched forward over the tops of both front seats. The duck girl went over the bandaged zombie- like man's left shoulder, then over the top of the steering wheel, and then through the left front windshield to the outside. The snake boy was methodically staying even with the duck girl, except that he went over the old man's right shoulder and then went out through the passenger window. From the window he began slithering like the snake he was, over the top of the exterior mirror and then back left onto the hood. I felt that everything was done so super slowly and methodically, in order for us to get that good look at the cloned creatures that we desired. We definitely got our money's worth watching them, as they wiggled and inched along toward the front of the hood. When the duck girl got onto the hood she began standing upright and inching along on her large webbed duck- like feet. The boy had begun stretching out his snake body as soon as his head cleared the mirror, and it appeared that the snake body was maybe at most six feet long and close to a foot in diameter. The girl's duck body alone was probably not more than 70-80 pounds and that is a non- scientific estimate only. The best part of the performance was yet to come when both creatures reached the one- fifth size bottle. Both of them reached out for the bottle in the same slow motion, and simultaneously. The duck girl reached ever so slowly around the bottom of the bottle with her tiny open left hand. At the exact same time the snake boy was reaching around the bottle just above her hand with his open right hand. They then reversed their journey and like pouring cold molasses, together they began sliding and inching their way back to the windshield. Finally back, they together slid the bottle right up against the right side of the windshield, directly over the rain drain vents and stopped. If they had pulled it an inch further it would have been on an unlevel surface and may have fallen off the car. The two of them then so slowly released their hands from the bottle simultaneously, and still evenly together, they slowly moved through the center of the windshield side by side. From the dash area each went back over the individual seats into the back rear seat. That ordeal of them retrieving that bottle from the front hood area, had taken more than twenty minutes while we had watched every move. After they had completed their mission, we were totally speechless and just stared at each other. It would prove to be another one of those times when not a soul appeared in my parking lot. Then for some unknown reason, that bottle would be left setting next to the windshield for a very long time. Finally around 8:30 pm, J went to the Subway to get some food for us since pizza still didn't sound good. I was in the office and it was not quite beginning to get dark yet. My door chimes rang and I saw a young fellow that I slightly knew coming in the door, and there was a slightly older unfamiliar man with him. The young fellow was a close friend of a full time employee, so he knew that unusual things had been happening at the store for a while. I called him by name and told him perhaps he would like to see some really weird stuff that had shown up in my car that evening. He and his friend looked at my car occupants on the front monitor, and instantly he wanted no part of going out to the car. However the friend got really excited about being able to see them up close, so the first man stayed at the rear of the car looking into the exterior mirrors. His friend walked up with me to the front passenger window beside the old man. He then looked into the back seat for several minutes and motioned for me to come back inside the store to talk. He was my first *messenger* of the day and it would lead me to a very important source in England during the following days. Ironically the friend had seen part of a science type special produced in Great Britain a couple of years earlier. The bottom line was that he had listened to some of the information from a former long time British M16 Agent, as he was discussing a long time joint U.S. and British cloning program on what he called "the dark side of the moon." I graciously thanked the younger man and his older looking friend for happening in to the store that night, because meeting that friend would prove to be one of those encounters created by God. J didn't leave until 2:00 Sunday Morning and the same four entities were still in the car and the bottle was still exactly where they had left it. When J left that morning, I walked her out to her car and then Sheba and I went back inside and locked up. I had earlier made the decision to stay overnight solely because of the bizarre creatures that were still in my car. I was pretty tired but the day's events still had my adrenaline pumping, so I decided to sit up a while and keep my eyes on my car. It was nearly 3am and somehow I had a feeling that I wasn't going to sleep anytime soon.

The constant question in my mind, as I watched the images of the four individuals on the monitor was; what kind of arrogant evil business operation would be marketing such revolting entities like those. Even more sick was; who would then put such creatures inside someone's automobile where they would be in front of several surveillance cameras. There would come a time soon, when I would discover the kind of arrogant organization that would be involved in such a business, which was cloning all kinds of sickening creations that must definitely be an abomination to God. I would also see firsthand that that same agency of our own government would try to destroy me, my family, my business, and literally anyone who tried to assist me in exposing the operation that they are involved in. I would also discover very soon that the first thing they try to do is always the same, they attempt to destroy the credibility of the messenger. Little did I know that

Sunday morning August 7, 2011, that I was less than twenty-four hours away from being the target of such an attempt? They intended to prevent my disclosure of the creatures which I had just discovered were being imported and exported from my property. I would discover that it was a top-secret agency of our government, which the taxpayers of this country support through their taxes. It would also turn out to be part of the same military that millions of us have been a part of. However more disappointing, would be that that government agency has withheld the truth, about what they have been deeply involved in for more than 60 years. Additionally, I would also learn that many well meaning citizens and officials, who have run afoul of the secretive operation, have been permanently silenced. The most telling part of the evil entities that had begun showing on Saturday August 6 would not be understood for a long while yet.

When I finally began understanding Biblical meanings of certain numbers, it would become so Biblically Prophetic who these entities were. The first ones were in my car on August 6 at Six PM, and the second batch appeared on Sunday August 7. The numbers 6 represents Satan and the number seven represents Spiritual Completeness, and Satan's direct hand on both days would be verified before that Sunday ended. My car was parked so that my front door camera as well as the two nearest cameras, were covering the area around the automobile. I was suddenly jolted out of my thoughts by what I saw coming out of my car. The trunk on my black Hyundai had just popped open, and out of it came a large grey and black Timber Wolf. As the wolf hit the ground I felt that I was asleep and dreaming but right away it became even more unbelievable. The wolf jumped around on the ground and then started milling around the back of the trunk. I got up and with Sheba beside me; we went to the front door where we would be within eight-ten feet of the car trunk, and I had my regular digital camera in my hand. There were two doors that were locked in the front doorway, and the inside door was a quite heavy glass door with a bar handle and it was locked at the top. My outside doors had been all special steel constructed seven months earlier after a costly break in. The outside doors were quite sturdy with heavy thick mesh grids that made it very difficult for anyone to see in from the outside. When we approached the doors, the wolf was standing at the outside door looking at us through the wire grid, so I unlocked and opened the heavy glass door. That left only the heavy wire mesh separating us from the wolf. The wolf appeared vicious but more than that, suddenly within two feet of the steel mesh door, the large grey wolf was quickly transfiguring into a seven-and-a-half-foot tall Beast. Supernatural Hybrids transfiguring from one form to another, was a phenomenon that I would encounter in more pronounced fashion, many times over the next 19 months. From that night forward, I would have that beast in my store, my vehicles, my home and barns until 12 noon on December 7, 2011. There would be times that I would have both the Beast and the Timber Wolf simultaneously around me. That same Beast was capable of becoming an alligator, and then a wolf, and then the seven and one-half foot tall man, who looked like he was in his middle to late 30s, and any variation in between. I would soon learn that the shape-shifting as it is called is more formally known as transfiguration, and it is a common ability to a certain group of individuals. It would become knowledge to me, that there are many individuals with transfiguration capabilities on this earth as well as in other worlds.

The Hybrids originally came from a sexual union between fallen angels and human females who were the descendants of Cain. The Flood in the Days of Noah was ordered by God, in order to rid the earth then of the Nephilem and Giants of those days. The descendants of those are called fallen angels or sons of God still today and their offspring are also called Hybrids, and many of them still have supernatural angelic powers in any number of ways. That event was my first encounter with the Hybrid shape shifters, but it would begin training me for more of them that were to come. It was 3:20 am when I first saw the trunk come open and it was now 3:40am. The Beast had a head so big, that you could have fit Sheba's big Rottweiler head inside of it. He was growling and snarling right up against the steel door not more than 12 inches away from my face. I had grown up to be a well schooled outdoorsman, and had hunted an assortment of dangerous game. I had never been as close-up to a head and mouth as large or to as many large sharp vicious teeth in my life. The Beast was drooling all over the outside concrete every time he opened his large mouth, and the growling was loud enough to be heard a good way off. The Beast had front paws as wide as a large dinner plate, when he grabbed the heavy iron mesh wire and began slamming the door back and forth against the frame. Sheba and I went back inside to my office and tried to record some pictures of him. Every time I clicked the mouse on him, he would roar and grab his upper body exactly precisely where I placed the cursor. He would react precisely as a big Grizzly shot with a rifle would react, he would sling his large head and front paws and grab at the perceived wound. I didn't realize yet because I would have thought it impossible, but the Beast was able to see exactly where I was placing the cursor on his body. It would be another month before I would begin to witness almost daily, that he could be in four distinctly different body forms. However, I never saw him in more than two different forms at the same time in one location. It would always be the Beast and the large Timber Wolf when I encountered two different forms simultaneously. I would assume that he was allowing one of the forms other than his bear form to see where I was placing the cursor on the screen, so he never had to move from the door to know everything that I was doing. I had a weapon there, but I knew that the beast was some kind of supernatural entity and that the weapon would be of no use. Yet, God would teach me later that the Hybrid shape shifters were mortal and could be killed. They always had to be killed at a time of day or night when their energy level was quite low.

With God's help, it would be possible for me to destroy seven (7) powerful supernatural Hybrid shape shifters over the period from December 2011 to March 2013, and seven represents Spiritual Completeness. Within another ten minutes, I saw six bright very white lights coming across my parking lot from west to east, and they were like 30-40-feet above my car. The white lights were each a small almost square aircraft of some type, and they were seemingly in an attached rectangular arrangement where they all moved and stopped at the same time. Then I saw small clusters of blue, green and red colored lights floating up out of my car into the bright white hovering squares over my car. The beast continued at the front doors slamming the 200-pound iron door against the building frame, while the small square-looking aircraft hovered overhead. All within maybe five minutes, the aircraft slowly moved away and out over the B farm property on the east side of my building. From there it lifted up and turned back to the north, and very slowly it disappeared out of sight. As soon as that happened the Beast disappeared, but for only a few minutes. I began looking closely at the monitors to determine what had happened with the hovering aircraft. It turned out to be the Beasts' job to safely get the creatures out of my car and into the small hovering aircraft and to keep me detached from everything that was taking place. It would become a nightly occurrence seven days a week at precisely 3:45am, those entities in my car or truck would be picked up by the unusual shaped drone-like aircraft.

Within a couple of days, I would learn many things about what and who was behind the operation which had chosen my property along I-44 as a safe place to bring in extra terrestrial entities. They would then hold them in my automobiles until they could be picked up in the early morning and taken to wherever they took them. There was someone on earth picking up the filth from other worlds after it was delivered to my property. Satan has been their boss for more than sixty years and Satan's own crews were delivering the ETs to my place. I now knew that this was the project that the *angel* meant when she said "God needs you to do something for Him, because of an ability that you have." Thankfully I have always had a God given knack for getting to the bottom of problems that others couldn't or wouldn't do, and not be afraid to do whatever it took to resolve it. The afternoon of August 6 I had realized that without a doubt, that what I was seeing in my car was literally from another world. Then Sunday night August 7 after two long days and night without rest, I realized that I was being attacked by several powerful enemies. However, it would be very soon that I would also start seeing help from the powerful hand of God. Miraculously, another previously unknown individual would show up in my life that who would really begin to provide me with priceless information about the evil ones who were involved. That *angel* who never gave me a last name would continue to visit me every two to three weeks for exactly two years, and then just as all the others I would never see him again. Now as I think back over the last twelve years, I know that he and all those other helpful people were "earth angels sent from God." Most of them like me were not sinless people, but just like me God was using them to carry out a plan. It seemed that each had a specific reason for appearing in my life, and once that reason had been accomplished, they would disappear. As strange as it was, most all of them would disappear and not be seen again. Not only would they not appear again, I would be unable to locate them or even know their true names. I learned to be able to sometimes recognize an individual as an "angel" by the manner in which they came in contact with me. Like the helpful old preacher on June 25, they would quite often acknowledge that it was a strange coincidence that got them to me. I will always cherish the memories of every one of them who appeared over the almost three years. As things got progressively wilder and much more treacherous, there were several times when strangers from other parts of the country had mysteriously appeared at the business. They would say that they had been sent from someone in locations like Davenport, Iowa to pray with the owner. There were two occasions when I wasn't there, and the strangers had asked two different employees if they would pray with them for me. So many anonymous people showing up to pray for a person they actually didn't know proved to me without a doubt, that God does work in mysterious and powerful ways. It was now 4:30 in the morning and I had seen and done a lot since 6 the evening before, but I was more drained emotionally than physically. I had witnessed the strangest things yet overnight with the Beast, but I was going to encounter an awful lot more. I really needed someone to talk to, so I decided to call my wife as I used to do to tell her of my latest ordeal. She didn't work outside of the home, and many times when she was alone she would stay up late. I realized what time it was, but what I was dealing with there was very shocking to put it mildly. She answered the phone and quickly told me, that I was seeing things and there was nothing like that there and she hung up the phone. I was making some coffee, because I certainly wasn't going to sleep and I had just started the coffee maker. I saw the Beast picture coming from one of the west parking lot cameras and he looked like he was coming around the corner of the building. Right after that, he appeared on the main front door camera again and was growling and slamming the door back and forth. That was exactly as had done earlier, and it was still an hour before daylight so I knew that I had to deal with him again. I had an idea that he was again trying to keep me inside the building again for some reason. Then he lumbered upright to the front east corner of the building, which put him maybe 60 feet from the area behind my front counter. We used a lot of heavy shiny steel hangers on the slat wall display areas. Behind the counter right next to where I sat, was where we kept a box with 100 to 150 or so of the extra hooks not being used, and together those hangers weighed as much thirty-five to forty pounds. Then as the beast started back toward my front door the metal hangers began jumping out of the box in handfuls at the time. I even put my hand over the top of the box and the hangers were bouncing against my hand pretty hard. I had never seen anything like it, but spiritually, that alligator, wolf, beast, man, was very powerful. We could see many things supernatural that he could do, such as in a room he could appear and cause several large plastic merchandise bags at once to fly up off of a desk. Instantly you would see and hear eye, nose and mouth holes pop open in the bottom of the bags at once like loud shots, and the bottom of the bags would resemble a bear's head sitting up on the desk staring at you. This time the beast was back at the front door looking in, as I began trying to record pictures of him again with my security cameras. Once again, he would growl and claw at every place on his body that I pointed the cursor to. The only pictures of him at the store that we would ever be able to save, would be one from the camera over the front door. I would get two frames of him changing back from the wolf then back into the alligator. That would be at 6:30 that that same Sunday morning just as my wife drove up and put her left foot on the ground. She would appear in the background of the picture with her foot on the ground as she exits the van, screaming there is no ######### bear here. Another time at my farm in late October, I would get three pictures with my digital camera at maybe fifty yards away through my living room window at 1:40 am. The beast was leading a swayback grey mare that was most obviously a ghost horse. I came home at 1am and was looking out the bedroom window at my car parked in the back yard, when he came out of a back pasture leading the grey ghost mare. The bear had fashioned a rope halter around the old mare's head and led her up to my opened rear car door.

I had called my wife again at 5:15 am that Sunday morning, and she had decided that she was going to drive the 52 miles up to the store. I didn't realize yet that nothing was ever going to convince her of all that was happening. During all the commotion caused by the beast, I had failed to notice that there were two individuals who were now sitting in my car. Meanwhile the Beast had changed back to the large timber wolf and loped across the west parking lot into the adjoining tire store complex, but he would be back before my wife would arrive. Now since it was getting daylight, I took Sheba and walked outside to check out the latest occupants in my car. I put Sheba on a leash after she ran around a bit, so that I could keep her close to me. Out of habit I had begun standing behind the vehicle and looking at the outside mirrors first before approaching close. This time I saw a well-dressed man in the driver seat and a witchy looking little woman in the front passenger seat. I then went on up to the car on the driver side and I looked into the cold black eyes of a most evil looking middle aged man. He was dressed in a bright camel colored two-piece suit and he had a quite expensive name brand gold with diamonds watch on his left wrist. He had a large stoned gold ring on his right hand. The man appeared to be very likely from a Middle Eastern country such as Syria, Iraq, Turkey or Lebanon. He had on a blue dress shirt with garnet colored cuff links, a dark garnet colored design tie and what appeared to be real alligator skin shoes. The man was well dressed to the point of being flashy and he seemed out of place just sitting in a stranger's car. The evil looking little woman barely weighed 90 pounds and she had small framed wire rimmed glasses, which didn't soften her looks a bit. She truly looked like a well dressed witch but she didn't look to be the same nationality as the man. The man was looking at me with the absolute meanest expression that I have ever seen. There were no expressions from either of them as I used my remote door lock flicker device to pop all four door locks open. Then I looked directly into his evil looking eyes as I reached out with my right hand and opened the driver door. He turned his head sideways to look at me as I said some less than nice things to him. As I spoke to him he always had a most arrogant very slight smirk on his face, and I felt something unusually evil about him that raised a big red flag. I had been in the presence of a hired assassin in another country a couple of times, and he was softer than either of the individuals in my car. I didn't know then who he was, but I knew that he projected a more evil aura than anyone I had ever seen. He looked like he had a really strong hate for me, and I really had no love for either of them either. More importantly, I truly didn't want either of them in my car, but I knew that they were in another dimension and I had no physical power over either of them. I would learn fairly soon that I could have power over him but only through a strong faith in God. I would prove to have been correct beyond a doubt, when I had determined that he was a very powerful supernatural enemy from some world or the moon. It would become evident to me a little further along, that he was the one in charge of all the cloned filth that was about to start arriving into my place in Missouri. I still didn't have the knowledge to understand how and why yet, that all the creatures were showing up in my vehicles. More important than anything else I would soon find out, was that this was only one facet of his evil forces that are throughout the world. Within the next week God would send another messenger with priceless information to me. There would be quite a few more messengers who would each contribute to my survival, and each one brought a special message.

It was August 7 and in five weeks God Himself was going to introduce me to that Evil One, in what would be the most spiritually powerful experience yet. I had realized that from the beginning incident in the tornado on May 22, every subsequent event seemed to grow more spiritually meaningful, but it also seemed that each successive enemy was more spiritually powerful. That next Biblical event would come, in the early morning hours of September 25 and would have me up close to that most undisputedly evil, spiritually powerful enemy in the world. That realistically spectacular event would allow me to witness for five straight hours, God's promise of of the Fourth, Fifth, and part of the Sixth Trump of God's End Time Prophecy in Revelations, which is the Final Chapter in the Holy Bible. However, it would still be almost two and one-half years before I would fully understand what I was to learn. I knew that I had things that I was going to do with all the special gifts of knowledge that He was giving me. I knew that it would forever be so difficult to realize, that I had been given so many awesome blessings. I had not truly included God in my life for many years, but I began in early August 2011 promising Him that I would tell the world about all the things that I was witnessing. The problem in getting that started was that I was involved in a battle that was to continue on and get progressively worse for a long time. It seemed as if I was living one day at a time, because each day seemed to get tougher. It was during those worst nights that I would constantly promise Him that I wouldn't quit, no matter how long it lasted or how bad it got. It had only gotten started at that time, and I had no idea that it would continue on in different forms for such a very long time. Even with all the disbelief coming from my wife and being passed on to my children, I still knew that I was without a doubt the luckiest man in the world. I realized that the things that were happening were so unusual, but I knew that it had to be truly God's Plan to show me these things for a specific reason. I began calling on God more as the times got worse, and in return my faith was being slowly strengthened. I could see even sometimes in the presence of others, how God was showing me that stronger faith allowed me to be able to rely on Him for everything. Even though some of my associates witnessed occasions when I had called on God in their presence, I never did it to impress them with my faith. Always before I called on God in the presence of others, I would tell them that it wouldn't be my strength that they would witness, it would come from God.

It was Sunday Morning August 7 and it was daylight and my wife was on the way to the store. I decided to attempt to take some pictures of the two evil looking individuals in my car. I had not forgotten the lesson from the evening before with the pictures not showing up. I took my older model digital camera out with me, and with Sheba beside me I took several pictures each of the man and woman. In watching the arrogant facial expressions of the two of as I snapped the pictures, I felt a little silly because I knew the pictures were not going to take just as well as they did. I didn't want to stay around them as I examined the pictures so I went back inside the store. I looked through all of the nine pictures that I took and I was way more than happy. I had taken four pictures of the female who I thought was a witchy looking, but well dressed woman. She was sitting in the front seat with her head facing toward the driver side where I was standing. I opened the driver door where the evil man was sitting and I took five pictures of him as he looked directly at the camera three feet away. The man allowed me to have one developed image out of the five which I took of him. Instead of a picture of him as he was sitting in my car, it was him in the exact same clothes but he was in a quite dark landscape with high power lines in the distance as far as you could see behind him. He was holding a small white cloned creature no bigger than a guinea pig, which was standing on the table in front of him. I couldn't determine with certainty but the face of the clone appeared doll-like. After J and I witnessing the cloned creatures the evening before, I knew that this was evidence of a cloning program outside of the U.S. by most likely our very own government. My immediate thought was that in his obvious arrogance, he was depicting himself spiritually holding that cloned animal as if in a show environment on the "dark side of the moon." The evening before I had been informed by a customer, of a documentary that he had recently saw on television. He described the show as producing credible evidence of a longtime illegal government cloning program, on what had been described as the dark side of the moon. He had told me about it immediately after I showed him the obviously cloned entities that had somehow been placed in my car. Then I made it a point that night to investigate it, and I learned that the dark side of the moon is the hemisphere which always faces away from earth. We never see that side of the moon, because the moon's rotational speed is about the same as the moon's orbital speed around the earth. You would have to be in space in order to see that hemisphere of the moon, I discovered. As for the man appearing in two places, I knew that only a spiritually powerful individual would have the ability to project themselves in two different locations simultaneously. However, I would see the same thing performed later by other extraterrestrials, and they would appear in a number of different settings. I would also have another just as awesome picture image, but it would be of the witchy looking woman in the car. I had always believed that witches were only mythical images of evildoers, which had been created for specific scenarios over thousands of years. However, there was one very clear picture that proved my belief had been wrong, and it developed from the four that I took of that little woman. The image was clearly a full length frontal picture of a female witch dressed in the customarily seen witch attire. She was dressed in a long black dress, large black cone shape hat, and black shoes. Surprisingly, her face appeared more pleasant looking in the black witch attire than it did in her regular looking clothes. Since the face looked quite different than the woman in the car, I oftentimes feel that in the black witch outfit she represented the persona which she was going to be in my life at that time. I will leave that thought right there without elaborating further, but it will always be a disturbing thought to me. Out of all the many entities that I encountered, I am still shocked every time I look back at that particular photograph and I realize that witches are real in some worlds, maybe even ours.

During my life, I had never given much thought to so call alien and UFO's reports from around the world. Even with the past experiences in an intelligence setting, I never knew anything about our government's involvement with extra-terrestrials from other worlds. Although I had always wondered why whenever someone made a report of a UFO sighting or an ET encounter, they would be labeled mentally unstable or else they would die mysteriously or disappear. Well, I was going to begin learning the answer firsthand, because I was never one to walk away from a bad situation when I knew I was right. My staunch resolve meant even when I had to face that problem alone, no matter how powerful the enemy was, I would not give in when I was right. Remarkably, the greatest thing that time would be that I knew God Himself was going to be with me, because I was involved in something that God expected me to finish. He began advising me in different ways and with every message that He delivered, it was as clear as if it was written on a blackboard. Most importantly, as the *angel* had promised on June 25, God would always do more than I asked of Him, and He would never forsake me. Looking back on those days and nights, I can promise you that God is way more awesome than most of us ever understand. Soon the next week, I would begin encountering other types of evil from that same world and others as well, but I would be blessed by the appearance of a most knowledgeable person who would step into my life.

It was 6 in the morning, as Sheba and I walked back into the store to make some coffee. Just as I turned on the coffee maker, there on the monitor was the big grey wolf standing behind the car. I watched on the cameras, as the beautiful 250-pound wolf changed into the beast. The Beast was standing up more than seven feet and one-half tall and was staring right at the interstate frontage road into my property. I immediately saw what he had been looking at, and it was my wife driving very fast toward my store in her grey van. I never knew if the beast knew who it was or not, but he quickly began changing back into the wolf. The wolf slowly began changing into a seven and one-half foot alligator lying on the ground directly behind my car. Many months later, I would discover two clear frames of the alligator at 6:30AM on August 7, 2011 on a surveillance cam log. It would be so unusual to find pictures of certain things on the logs from those many months of unusual daily occurrences. My surveillance camera operation would be hacked by sophisticated means, and they would be remotely turned on and off hundreds of times. I believe that God Himself, had saved numerous high value pictures from the surveillance logs, that otherwise would have been destroyed or stolen. We were able to find a good number of similarly important pictures hidden in files in the computers. The pictures, which had all been taken by the outside cameras, were found hidden in different factory installed programs on my security system computers. I hired a quite knowledgeable computer technician to work on the computers, and he told me that it would be difficult to hide those images in that manner. Nevertheless, I still tell people that among all of His supernatural abilities, God is also the best expert on any technology; because after all, He created the technology. It was 6:30 AM when my wife put her left foot on the ground as she got out of her car, according to the time as recorded by the outside cameras. I have loved my wife dearly and trusted her with my life for more than forty-five years, but I have never totally understood her reasoning for what happened next. She began screaming at the top of her lungs on that otherwise quiet Sunday Morning, there is no ########## bear and you know it. As she was screaming and walking toward the back of the car, the alligator vanished totally into the trunk of my Hyundai, and I watched it all. What I didn't yet understand, was that the most all of the Hybrids would have varying degrees of supernatural abilities. It would become quickly evident in my 24/7 contact with him, that this Hybrid was a most awesome spiritually powerful individual. In all forms, he would become my worst nightmare for exactly four months from the date of August 7th, and I would personally watch him become transfigured probably more than 50 times. I would have to deal with the most unbelievable events created by that creature, and within the next week God would tell me who he was working directly under. The beast would continue making my life Hell, because God was allowing those things to test me. He was always there when I needed Him, because without His being there during those days and nights, I would not be alive today. My wife had parked a distance from my black car, which was in front of the door slightly to the east side. As she began walking up to the store the alligator had disappeared from my view. What I didn't yet understand was that the alligator was now the Timber Wolf, and that he was curled up inside my trunk on a blue tarp that I kept there. During those days my wife and I both had keys to each vehicle that we owned, so her plan was to use her key to take the car home. She came up to the front door of the car arguing with me that there was nobody in the front seat, as I watched both of the evil ones as they rolled their eyes at me. She definitely intended to drive the small car home to Oklahoma right away and leave her van there for me. I had another Ford Escort that stayed at the store also which had belonged to my son while he was in college. I traded him another pickup that I had, so that I would have an extra car there all the time. My wife was only intent on driving the black car home with the two entities in it, and because of a discerned unknown fear I was begging her not to. I truly knew that there was something really evil in that car and I begged her not to take it. In the past she would never have tried to go around me in that manner, but that morning she was like I had never seen her before. Unfortunately I would begin seeing that and worse come out from her interactions with me. I even started to physically hold her back, but I knew that she was going to cause a really bad scene out in public view, and I never wanted to physically harm her. I can today say for a fact, that my wife of forty plus years was at least temporarily possessed, by that powerful evil force in my car. The plan whether symbolic or not, was for her to take that car with the two evil entities in it to our home. I begged and pleaded with her that something really bad was in that car, and I truly screamed at her, but all to no avail. That would prove to be a truly sad moment in my family's life after all those years, when she drove away from the store that Sunday morning. As she was getting in and adjusting the front seat, I could see the man in the camel suit behind her in the seat, looking at me in such an evil face. Amid much screaming and profanity, she spun away in a cloud of gravel and dust toward the interstate. I quickly went back inside and made up a Temporary Closed sign for the door, and got into her car to try again to stop her from going through with her plan. I was literally going crazy because I just knew that she had made a most horrendous mistake, and time would prove me so very correct. In hindsight I wish that I had disabled the car before she got there that morning. I will never be able in this world, to undo all the evil and vile things that were put in motion that Sunday Morning. What was done that morning would not only hurt her, but would help lead to the death of our beautiful and caring twenty seven year old daughter. It would bring on many different evils that would be more powerful than I can ever relate to you. I have never understood whether it was meant to be symbolic by God or not, but that evil in my car would bring a more destructive atmosphere to my home than anyone could ever imagine. I would understand in a little more than a month what was in my car that day, which she brought to our home. Within five minutes after she left I was in her car and following and trying to catch up with her. She was already on the west side of Joplin when I caught up to her along I-44. I pulled alongside of my black Hyundai at about 70 miles per hour, and I tried hard to get her to look over at me. The man in the camel suit reached around my wife and put his left hand on the dash, and I could clearly see his eyes as he looked at me with that arrogant glare. The mean looking little witch on the other side looked over at me over her wire rimmed glasses with a "so what you going do now ?." My wife wouldn't pull over or talk to me at all and she went on to the farm. I knew that if I followed her she may have a wreck trying to get away from me, so I turned around and regretfully drove back to my store. It wouldn't be long before the evil would get cranked up in my house, and it would go nonstop for a very long time. I knew that I had unusually strong reservations about the individual in my car, which was hell-bent to take to our home. My greatest fears would become reality very soon, when I would understand who the man in my car was.

I drove back to the store and opened it back up, and as usual Sheba was exceptionally happy to see me and I really needed that. Sheba would be my constant spiritual reinforcement so many times over the next several years of my life. I thought long and hard about what had appeared in my car the last two days, and there was no doubt that it was crazy stuff, and it was all real. I decided to do something that would reflect how truly naïve I was at that time about the government's denial and concealment of the extraterrestrial existence. I made what seemed to be a logical decision to contact law enforcement and tell them what was going on. I had had a relationship with FBI personnel many years before, and had found it to be a well respected agency of federal law enforcement. I didn't think local law enforcement was the right choice, and later that would prove to be a correct decision shortly. When I made the decision to contact the FBI I truly believed that I was possibly alerting them to some kind of national security risk like I had never seen. Since I had a bit of knowledge in that field, I will never forget my shock at the irresponsible demeaning response, that I was met with that afternoon from the FBI office in Kansas City, Missouri. When I called, I clearly identified myself as a long time businessman, and gave the woman my age because I realized what I was going to report sounded unusual. I wanted them to know that I was anything but crazy, so I purposely avoided using any trigger words like aliens or such. I just told her that I had some very unusual persons who had appeared in my car while it was parked at my business. I then told her that my wife had driven that car home to just inside Oklahoma, with the two persons still in the car. She asked me what they looked like and I remember saying, they probably were not from our world. At that point she said and I quote her exact statement to me "we don't do aliens and we don't do ghosts." I then began trying to give her a little background on myself, as she quite rudely hung up the phone. I thought to myself, I don't believe that woman in the FBI office just talked to me like that. So I decided to call back and a different woman answered the call, and I told her what just had happened and I also ask her not to hang up the phone. I told her that I had some background in common sense and had a fair amount of education as well. I also gave her a contact to call and check my word out for credibility. It did seem that this woman believed me so I was able to tell her more about it, and I even offered the employee's name that was with me the night before. That lady found that I lived in northeast Oklahoma so she told me to call Tulsa FBI Office, which I did that same afternoon. An agent was to call me the next day for a meeting somewhere to discuss, but that call never happened. There was a reason that it didn't happen, and it further proved that the FBI and all the other law enforcement agencies were involved in another ET-UFO cover up. That was something that I I had never heard of whenever I contacted them initially that afternoon. I was certainly about to learn how serious the cover up operation would become at any cost, after I got home that afternoon around 5:30. The agent in Tulsa had also asked me to call the local sheriff department in my home county in Oklahoma that afternoon, until he and I could talk on Monday. I was totally naïve about the organized deception and lies surrounding anyone who tries to report either a UFO or the ET's as I did. What would really begin disgusting me would be the extent to which the government's secret operation would infringe on my rights and my life. The fact was that I didn't go on government property to find all the filth, yet it had literally taken over my property and business operation. I didn't know yet how dangerous my life was going to become, until I began talking about the creatures that were appearing on my business property, in my vehicles, home, barns, etc. I was going to get educated real fast as things began unfolding at my farm that evening, when the county deputies got to my house at 6.

The two county deputies had just driven to my place from the county seat 25 miles away, and the Sheriff himself was even on the way. They walked up and the one in charge asked me, where were the people who were in my car? When my wife came home, she had backed my car up beside an Oak Tree in the side yard. I had walked over to my car as soon as I got home and looked at the two individuals in it. They were still just as arrogant as they had been earlier that morning. The deputy and I walked to within 10 feet of the car and he stopped, but I walked right up to the car window on the driver side. As I did that, the two entities looked straight ahead, but were seemingly conversing in some manner to each other. They knew the rouse that I was caught up in with the cops, because I would later many times watch how adult ETs would react when a non-believer couldn't see them. I told the head deputy, that it was the same man and woman in the car as earlier in the day, and both were sitting in the front seats. He told me that he couldn't see them but that he needed to make a phone call. He called someone other than the Sheriff, because he was still on his phone when the Sheriff drove up in my yard. The Sheriff then called the head deputy to get in his car with him, and he called someone else and I could see much discussion going on. The Sheriff even backed his car further away from where I was standing, as if I may hear the conversation. At that point I knew that the Sheriff was calling the government handler who had taken charge of the deception activity. During all the secret discussions between the cops, she never got involved in them or said anything to me. It had become a painful thing already, to watch my wife of 40 years and the mother of my children, to turn against me in such an obvious conspiracy.

I had already caught on when my first call to the FBI was abruptly disconnected. So as I watched it all unfolding that evening at my home, I made a vow to myself that I was not going to lay down for any of them. I knew that I was being 100% truthful and I never quit anything when I knew was right. Even to this day I offer to take properly administered polygraphs as to everything that I contend in this book. I knew that the U.S. Government believed highly in polygraphs, but I knew that they wouldn't ever rely on them unless they controlled a situation.

The morning after the emergency room charade, the first thing bright and early I was in the Miami Integris Hospital Office. I had an appointment with the psychiatric doctor in charge of that hospital and the Grove Hospital from the night before. We sat down and she pulled up the other so-called doctor's paperwork from the emergency room the night before. She was quite shocked and unhappy at what she read on that paperwork. She asked me some questions and we had discussions about the entire scenario. In summation the doctor in charge said that I only appeared very tired and quite stressed from something. I agreed with her, but she couldn't even imagine how much sleep I had lost during late May, all of June and July. Now I had lost all of Saturday night's sleep and was up all day Sunday until quite late, and I certainly didn't instantly fall asleep Sunday night. As for the diagnosis from Grove Hospital, the psychiatric specialist in charge said about the emergency room doctor in her own words was: "that he had no training, no authority, nor the ability to make such a diagnosis. In other words he had no training as a psychiatric physician. She told me that she saw nothing that empowered her to do anything except make some suggestions. She suggested that I must get more rest, but that was something that I wouldn't be able to do for another couple of years. Their mental incompetence attempt had struck out that time, but buoyed by my wife's participation with them, they would become much more aggressive in their attempts to totally discredit me with a number of other agencies, federal, state and county.

My wife was also contacting everyone that she knew I had a relationship with, in an attempt to discredit me. My wife had told people the month after the Joplin tornado, that I was suffering from PTSD and then within another three months, she was telling people that I had to be taking delusional or hallucinogenic drugs. We had for many years sold several varieties of energy type drinks and powders, of the same brands that the quick stops and truck terminals sold. They were totally harmless and were no different than the popular brands of energy supplements that had been around for years. I had purchased various energy supplements for the probably the last 15 years of my life, because they gave me energy and also kept me awake driving. As a matter of coincidence, the energy products business was owned and managed by a retired former U.S. Drug Enforcement Agent, who I considered a good friend-associate. At the time, I had also fully apprised him of the government's ET and cloning program, which was utilizing my Portal location to bring their mixed human- creatures in. He and his associate were leaving my store late one night just at midnight in late 2011, and I had my car and truck parked side by side in front of the store. I pointed out to him in both of my vehicles, that there were a number of very weird looking individuals. All of those entities in both the vehicles were waiting to be picked up before daybreak that next morning. He was one of many people who knew and saw, the things that were being dropped into my property every night against my will.

I was about to learn that the agency was bringing in the various types of cloned entities nightly, through the Portal which was along the west edge of my property. Extra terrestrials of many different types were escorts, who accompanied the young clones of humans crossed with mammals, fowls, snakes and once several human fish. It was all being delivered into my vehicles, after arriving from some location by way of the Portal. The new groups would begin appearing in my vehicles every night of the week, by midnight. Then each morning beginning at 3:45 AM promptly without fail, the super white lighted government operated specialty drones would slowly float into and slightly above my parking lot. There was always at least one vehicle parked in the front parking lot, even if none of us were at the store. I had an older model Ford

Escort that was parked in the parking lot at all times. However, when I was there, they always chose to use my personal truck or car or both. We also have many pictures of the entities being picked up out of one of my employee's car. The drones would hover over the autos at 25-30 feet and the assorted entities would float right up into the brightly lit orb- like compartments. The bright white cubicle orbs seemed to serve several purposes, it provided a definite hiding place for the now very small entities, as well as the bright white lights provided recharging for the entities. I have many pictures of from three to as many as eight of the pickup cubicles hovering on different early mornings over my parking lot. I never knew where they were taking the creatures, but they always went back in the direction which they had come from. I did get probably reliable information that they were not taking them back more than 12 miles from my location after they were picked up. The quite small orb-like drones were remotely controlled without a doubt, and they looked as if they were mechanically connected in a block shape of one to eight at the time. I watched them numerous mornings beginning precisely at 3:45 am overhead at only 25-30 feet above the cars, as we photographed them manually from within 20 feet. It became necessary to manually take the photographs of the entities being picked up, because the ETs running the operation began remotely shutting down all of my surveillance and security system. That began on Tuesday morning August 9 at 3:30 am and continued seven days a week over the next five months, until December 9, 2011. All of the surveillance system would then stay off until 5:30am, and the most obvious reason for them shutting it off was to prevent my cameras from filming the pickups. When the plans were drawn up originally for the operation, no one expected me to know about the operation, because I went home each night after midnight closing. I would determine late on Monday night August 8, that the shape-shifting Beast was the main security in charge of the onsite pickups each morning. The two bosses who were over the Beast were going to show up very shortly and they would be like something out of a science fiction-horror show nightmare. They would be my constant worse enemy around my property, while they always sat in one of my vehicles. It would be a long time before I would truly know what they were. God would tell me that they were frog looking demons with Elliptical eyes that burned bright green in total darkness. They are mentioned in Revelations as frog-like demons.

As the configuration of small yellowish cubicles crossed over into my west parking lot, we could see the tinker toy type connectors between each of the cubicles. Once the remote-controlled cubicles stopped in place above the vehicles, they slowly became an extremely bright whiter color. As the lighted cubicles became brilliantly whiter, they took on an oblong orb fuzzy appearance. Then as the entities flew up into each orb, it appeared that they were divided into the cubicles separately for some reason. Once the entities entered the super white orb, they would no longer be distinguishable. I learned that entities that were seven and one-half feet tall the previous night, would become as small as a bumble bee by 3:45 am, and they would stay small for hours as they recharged. One morning there may be six cubicles connected with three rows of two, and the next morning there may only be three total cubicles connected when they arrived. It appeared to be representative of how many different entity groups were being picked up from my cars. I could tell that when there was more than one distinct type of entities, it appeared that they tried to separate the different groups of entities by where they came from. The reason I had made that finding, was because each group would have different escorts that I called strong arms. The strong arms would sometimes be powerful cloned individuals themselves, or they would be extraterrestrials of many different types. There was definitely a mixed type of extraterrestrials who were each bringing in different type clones. I felt that the adult ETs that were with the young cloned creatures were representative of different alien species, due to the many different physical appearances. Also,

I got that same opinion from a much better informed person who I had met in December 2011. Most of the ETs that were escorting the cloned entities appeared to be in their upper teens to maybe thirties. The younger guards would often be in the company of one or more, older looking rough and spiritually powerful ETs. Also, it seemed that the more valuable cloned creatures would have the toughest appearing guards escorting them. It was also obvious that the escorts were coming from very different areas due to their physical characteristics. It felt that many of the ETs were coming out of another dimension not too far away, but I never had any proof of that.

◆◆◆◆◆

I would soon begin reciting the old Watergate investigation statement made in those days by G. Gordon Liddy, another former CIA Operative. He would say "if your government is trying to kill you, tell the world, and if you are killed the world will know that your government killed you." Liddy also had another truth that I embraced, which I had espoused and witnessed all of my adult life. That saying was" tough times that don't kill you , but will only make you stronger." I began telling a number of people who I trusted about the secret government operation that I was accidentally being overrun by. Some of those notified were in high places associated with Washington D.C., and others were respected individuals with ties within UFO and Extra Terrestrial disclosure groups. In 2000, U.S. Senator Jim Inhofe of Oklahoma had nominated my son for an appointment to U.S. Naval Academy. I have always felt that Mr. Inhofe was a good and decent man, and I knew that he had some connections within the governmental agencies. For those reasons, in the fall of 2011 I contacted his office in Washington for assistance with what was taking place in my life, which I understood was most likely a secret operation by an agency of U.S. Air Force. I wanted him to understand the very real nightmare of the havoc, which an agency of our government was twisting into every part of my life. By that time in the fall of 2011, I had also learned firsthand, that our government would do anything in order to conceal its involvement in such operations. Not surprisingly, Senator Inhofe let me down, like others he didn't have the guts to investigate what I honestly had reported to him. Inhofe didn't want to acknowledge the governments participation in the alien cloning coverup.

Then in 2012, we began getting an occasional surveillance image of blue military vehicles, once at an unusual hour of the morning. However, the vast majority were private cars with base identifying stickers on them coming in and out of the property. Pictures were recorded of two well-marked Air Force Blue military cars, which were parked in my lot on different days. A plain clothed individual once parked an official U.S. Air Force vehicle, almost directly in line with my front door cameras, and a couple of other times there were parked official vehicles in the west side parking lot. We would eventually begin getting five to 8 visits per week from mostly four specific states. This forced us to start walking outside and getting tag numbers and base ID from vehicle stickers. I felt pretty sure that we were getting mostly Level 2 and 3 personnel that were appearing most frequently. Level 3 would have been top secret also, but would likely only be the black project cover up for the Level 2, which were the so called Black Ops units. Level 1 would have been the select few who fully knew everything about the ETs and the cloning program. I am almost certain there was at least one Level 1 person, possibly an NSA official from a state well northeast of Missouri, like Area 51 where I had documented two unit members from the same Air Force base, positively being identified coming into the property in one week. Over the months ahead, we would discover that four specific U.S. Air Force bases, seemed to be sending the vast majority of personnel to my business location. I could usually pick them out by their demeanor as they came in the front door, if not it would be their exaggerated gazing at the inside of the building. Frequently they would take pictures around the three acre property as they drove in or out of my parking lot. I once watched an individual from a Nevada military base, as he was filming the area as he drove in along the I-44 frontage road. Then he continued filming the entire acreage and buildings from the very front of the parking area. One of us would usually go outside and verify their vehicle, stickers, tags or documents often lying in plain view inside the car. By the spring of 2012, there would be a minimum average of one documented military individual per day actually coming into the store. They had an air about them that I could pick up on, so I began asking them for ID when I was working or if I was in the store, when they came in. I eventually also had two associates who became able to identify some of them as military, when they came in the store. Initially they would provide identification, which most times would only be a state driver license, but sometimes it would tie back to identification on the car. I would not let my employees decide who to ask for ID unless I was in the store, then I usually went outside and looked around the vehicle to be sure I was correct. It was amazing the kinds of drawings and notes that I observed lying open in the seats and on the dash of vehicles. Amazingly in 2012, I had an older gentleman who came in and he turned out to be a retired military officer. After I made my case of what I was being subjected to, along with my telling him a little about myself, he confessed to me that he was aware of what was drawing so many military personnel to my property. By those times, I already had tons of proof, interaction and understanding of whom and what was driving it all.

In the second week of August 2011, I learned what the foggy lighted area was, that was visible at night on the west side of my property. Even though I couldn't see it every night, it was quite visible on clear nights. I had only shown it to two trusted associates during the last week of July, even though I had been observing it off and on for more than a month. A well qualified person who I had only met three times over the last two months, stopped in at my business one evening around 10:30pm. J was off that night and I had another model that had been working, but it was slow, so I had let her off. I knew that my visitor lived two states away and that he had retired from a specific special operations unit of one of the military branches. I had learned earlier from him that he had a business east of Missouri, and that my store was on his route back and forth to that location. He knew a little of my past as I did his, because we had discovered that we were in a similar place at the same time many years earlier. That night in August when he came into my store, it was a clear evening and business was so slow that I was thinking of closing early. We had barely exchanged greetings, when he asked me how things were going with the spirits that I had told him about. I had told him about what was going on with us, on the morning of the Fourth of July when he had last been there. Before even telling him what had happened on August 6, I told him I was first going to close up for the night and we could better talk. We walked outside and I let Sheba run around while we sat on the tail gate of my truck. Without me saying anything, he saw me looking at the foggy dimly lighted area towards the west of my lot. He asked me if I knew what I was seeing over there. I told him that I didn't know what it was, but I knew that it had appeared shortly after the Joplin Tornado. It so happened that night that the area was more clearly defined than I had ever noticed before. I told him that I had really been wondering what it was for some time. He began telling me things that I had never ever heard in my life about the dimensional Portal that had appeared on my property shortly after the Joplin Tornado in May. I told him what had happened to me over the previous weekend with the entities in my car, and about my calls to the FBI, and my trips to the hospital. Since R as I will call him, hadn't made motel reservations ahead I offered to let him stay there that night. He would turn out to be one of those gifts that I was continuing to receive from literally strangers appearing in my life.

Earlier in the week after the last weekend, I had begun searching for two different individuals who I wanted to talk with about what I had encountered. So far I had not reached either of them, but this man was more than I needed to begin understanding what I was up against. I will not disclose a specific of anything which may identify him, because he did for me was what he felt was the decent thing to do. Having been involved in similar operations, he could tell me what was going to happen in my episode going forward. I also firsthand witnessed and learned many things that most people reading this story will not believe, but I know them to be true firsthand. Senator Inhofe's office manager seemed most helpful in listening to my problem. She explained that many times when the Senator would question an operation, the government agency involved would stonewall him for as long as possible. She promised me that she would personally address my complaint with the Senator as quickly as possible. Meanwhile, she said the Senator may have a qualified representative from the Tulsa office come over to Missouri to check out the complaint. The illegal government operation continued seven days a week and I never was contacted back from anyone in either of the Senator's offices. After several months I contacted his office again, and was told that the government was be claiming that I was part of some kind of investigation that they were conducting. I did know that they were trying very hard to frame me up on anything that they could, just to take away my credibility. That had always been the initial modus operandi, when someone had come forward with claims of experiences with UFO or ETs. I believed right up front that cloning of humans - animals in any manner was against the law in the United States and that the cloning was taking place well away from the U.S. In late summer of 2012, I again contacted the Senator's Tulsa office, since they were all on summer recess in Washington. I spoke with a male office manager who again promised assistance and the complaint would be seriously looked at. To this day, I have never ever gotten any kind of response from

Senator Jim Inhofe, concerning the unbelievable wrongdoing that was perpetrated by government employees against me. However in his defense, I understood well how the government uses what they call "the onion skin effect" to shield top secret operations. They will allow the persons such as U.S. Senators, who provide funding to the programs, to only have knowledge of what is on the black level which covers the hidden program. I had pretty fair knowledge of what to look for and was able to detect all sorts of electronic surveillance. It was being run on my cell phones, office phones, computers in my office and home, business surveillance system, and even on both vehicles. The unlawfulness, to which their cover up operation would stoop, would be unlike anything that I had ever heard of. I saw many persons ignoring the fact of what was taking place nightly on my business property in Missouri. I once had two county deputies in my parking lot one morning right at 3:45am, just as the pickup drones were coming into my west lot. When I showed them the drones; one deputy said to the other;"let's get out of here that's some kind of government stuff." They had both listened as I pointed out how the drones blended into the lights along the interstate, and I had explained exactly where they would cross over I-44 to my property. One does not spend most of their adult life in Washington politics, and not know that our government has been in bed with the ETs for more than 60 years. It is one of those issues that take real guts to stand up against it, so most politicians and others choose the easiest path by just ignoring the evidence. From a personal perspective, it is a most cruel act to deny truth because you have no backbone to support the claimant. I believe those who knowingly ignore the truth of the half century long government ET cover up, are themselves also guilty of bearing false witness against the victims. I will stand up for what is right even when I have to stand alone, and most times it takes a lot of backbone. By the Grace of God, I inherited that trait from a long line of ancestors.

There would be a real irony in me uncovering and witnessing the government's cloning program. When I was a young boy growing up I realized that my dad was more than just highly intelligent. I also knew that he seemed to have an uncanny perception of things that were to come, even many years after his death. I enjoyed asking him questions about a variety of subjects, because I knew that he would always be totally confident in his answers. Once when I was maybe ten to 11 years old, I had asked him what he thought might happen in the world one day that God would be the most displeased with. I would never have ever remembered that conversation again, had it not been for my uncovering of vivid disturbing evidence of our government's involvement in cloning humans with animals, fish, fowl and snakes. On August 6, 2011 when I realized that I and an employee were clearly witnessing a human-duck and a human-snake clone in my car at my office, that conversation with my dad and his answer flashed clearly into my head. I vividly recalled his answer to me that day 54 years earlier which was; that he believed that God would be most unhappy when people began breeding humans with other kinds of creatures. I truly believe God had allowed my dad to appear at my business on the nights of July 9 and 16 in 2011, in order to jar my memory of that specific conversation from many years ago. Those occurrences together were all planned by God, to alert me that the cloning program was part of what the *angel* had meant when she said "it is an ability that you have for something that God needs you to do." I had then asked my dad how humans and animals could ever be interbred. His answer was that one day a way would be likely be discovered that would make it possible. We saw the two cloned entities on August 6, but by December 8 I had seen many more humans cloned with several other types of animals and even a fish, that was likely a swordfish.

On Monday August 8, 2011 I went to the Miami Integris Hospital in Miami, Oklahoma. The female doctor in charge of the psychiatric unit was openly quite critical of the actions of the emergency room doctor from the night before. Her advice to me that I needed more rest would have to go unheeded for a long time to come. With the things that our government was going to be bringing into my property nightly, I could not allow myself the luxury of sleep. I would have been a worthless, irresponsible person if I had ignored the things that were going on in my store, automobiles, and my home and barns in Oklahoma. I knew they were all real and nobody anywhere was going to disprove my allegations if I lived through it. In the event that I didn't make it, I was providing a number of select individuals with lots of specific information surrounding the Hell that I was being put through.

I left the hospital that morning and drove the twenty-five miles back to my house. I got ready and left for the trip to work in Missouri by 3 that afternoon. J was coming in at 4, and since she hadn't talked to me since leaving Saturday morning around 2, she had no idea of the Hell I had been through. I was expecting to be contacted back from a British source for more information on the cloning program expose several years earlier. Thankfully, it was going to happen later in the week, as well as the visitor who would bring word that the Portal on my property was going to be a lightning rod for the government. The greatest part would be his explanations of how certain things would start to happen and who would be behind it all. I had already begun experiencing some of what he would warn me of, but there were going to be more serious threats just ahead. It would amaze me as to how many different agencies, would become involved in trying to create problems in my life. I got in to work and I let C go home at 2:45 without me telling her anything about the weekend happenings. I got my keys out and unlocked my office door, and it hit me like a ton of bricks what I was seeing. J and I had been so tied up with everything happening Saturday afternoon and evening, that we had totally forgotten the seven remaining spiritual people who were still in the building. I had not even told J at all Saturday, what had happened with them and me Friday night before I closed.

We didn't even notice that they were not there Saturday evening, nor did I remember seeing them all night Saturday or Sunday either. There inside my locked office, was a note of sorts from the seven beautiful people who had spent their last summer with us. A clear spiritual form of each one of them was there in my office, and each one was wearing an outfit that I recognized. One of the two lovely women, who had always put the basket of faded roses into my pictures, was there but the other one had already left two weeks ago. I grabbed my cell phone out of my pocket and started taking what would their last pictures. They were all appearing as if children taking a pleasant nap, while in chairs and sitting on shelving in two places in the office. Not more than 20 seconds after I started attempting to take their pictures, every one of the entity forms disappeared simultaneously. I sat down and began looking through my phone for the several pictures that I had taken. I thought I had snapped a picture of each group of them, but only one picture appeared and I will always cherish it. There was a blue quart size milk carton that said on one side; "Got Milk? On the other side that was visible, it said; Got Friends? That picture summed up a lot of memories of a short summer with some of the most beautiful friends, but I had a strong feeling that we would all meet again one day.

Before J got in at 4, I wanted to sit down at my desk and sort through surveillance camera logs from Sunday overnight. I had not had anyone come into the store since I got in, but as I sat down to check the log I saw a very strange sight on the west lot cameras. There was an Indian ceremonial performance just beginning very close to the southwest corner building. It was exactly 3:30pm when it started and the performance would last until 5:30 that afternoon. We would begin watching the same daily performance seven days a week from that date forward. There would also be hundreds of randomly appearing activities by different Indian Spirits that would continue until late in 2013, when I permanently would close the business down. The 3:30pm every day ceremonies would continue until the 8th day of December, which would be the day the cloned entities would abruptly stop coming in and out of my property. The day before, on December 7, 2011 the Grizzly Hybrid would finally be destroyed, after he began attacking me as I drove south on Highway 71 below Neosho, Missouri. He would be killed that day at Noon as I drove through Anderson, Missouri. That Monday afternoon, I was still totally engrossed in watching the mysterious tribal performance when J came in at 4. She went and got her lingerie display together and came back in my office. Together we watched and discussed what we were seeing, until precisely 5:30 when it ended for the day. Little did we know, but the afternoon dances were going to continue daily as long as the human-animal clones kept coming. Each ceremony would always finish up with the dramatic conclusion of a beautiful Eagle Dance. The performance always ended when an Eagle Feather adorned dancer wearing a large pair of eagle wings, would suddenly collapse with his quite large wings outstretched and facing down. As the performance ended, I began updating J on all the things that had happened since 2am Sunday when she left. She was shocked at the attempts by my wife and the government handlers, to get me committed to a mental facility. I also told her about the administrative doctor in Miami that morning, and how she had definitely shot that down temporarily. I assured her that things were going to get much worse for me, because I wasn't planning to back away from the truth. It was difficult for her to understand why people didn't want to accept the reality of extraterrestrial ties that our government had. At that time I had only begun learning how hard the government would work to prevent the truths from coming out. Much later in 2013, J would come back to work for me, and she would have a hard time believing how many things they had done to me for so long. J was going to be target for them because she was such a laid back type of person, and she had a way of being quite convincing. Just as I would find out over the next several days, the program plan for the government would be to move her out of the way in the not too distant future. Their customary procedure would be the same every time later, when I gained a new loyal associate and witness. It would take pretty strong individuals, to withstand the numerous disguised forms of harassment against them. Because of the government's goon squads, as time went on I would have fewer and fewer regular partners who could take it. I would see attacks coming over the next two years from an assortment of county, state, and medical providers. I watched the secret federal agency as they went to county officials, in order to target a couple of my key employees over senseless things. They would stoop so low as to hire anonymous deadbeats, to place false ads falsely accusing me of any number of vague things. I was going to be made aware that this would be the normal modus operandi from my enemies, so I got used to it. Yet, no one ever wants to be constantly falsely accused, so it took a lot of self restraint to handle it. Without God, I could have never been as strong and patient as I was against so many constant threats coming from every direction. I always said that I would have much rather preferred being in a real shooting war, because at least I could have shot back at the enemies. They wanted to destroy me or my credibility, and they didn't care in what order it was. I knew from past experience that our government had always placed much credence in their polygraph tests. I had always asserted that I would be more than happy to submit to a properly administered polygraph, to the truthfulness of anything that I ever contended concerning the events taking place. At this time twelve years later, I still make that same offer to verify my statements about anything that I allege.

I explained to J that Monday afternoon, how the beast had appeared to be keeping me inside the building after she left Sunday morning. I thought about it later Sunday morning, and I realized that he was trying to keep me from interfering with the orbs which were picking up the entities out of my car. Based on that conversation, J was going to stay over Monday night to see what would transpire. We had a slow Monday night businesswise, but we had a great evening discussing much of what was going on. We were seeing something about the size of a bumble bee that was flying in and out of the building, as it got closer to closing time. I didn't yet understand that it would be the Beast, because he would be interested in watching everything that we were doing. We began seeing the same scenario every night before closing, but it would be several more days before God would totally enlighten me to the strengths and weaknesses of all the supernatural enemies. I had watched the friendly spirits earlier in the summer, as they taught me that we all have the ability to fly in the spirit world. I was going to learn that even the most supernatural of spirits, became very small and weak at a point during every twenty-four period. I would also understand directly from God that they all became very vulnerable at that point, since they would be in their weakest form. They would become much easier to actually destroy at that time, and that was why I would find that they tried to hide away at that time every night. Prior to learning that, I would have no inkling of how small that normally large Grizzly would become, late each night. That would be another one of those many awesome things, which God would only be just beginning to teach me. God showed me how to locate the charging areas that the entities would utilize in order to be recharged.

We closed at midnight and sat around and talked about all the unusual paranormal things that were appearing on all of the cameras. During those days and nights, together we were taking more than 50-100 pictures every twenty-four hours, not counting the surveillance cam images. In those times, the outside cameras were taking sometimes more than one hundred per night. Since those cameras were all motion activated, they were taking some unusual images at all hours of the night. Fortunately, many of us had started taking many pictures manually, because on the 30th day of December, 2011 the modem from my surveillance computer would disappear. That same thing would happen every six-month period through 2012. There was no doubt as to who was behind the cowardly thefts, because it was the same deep state agency that was remotely taking control night and day of my entire surveillance system. That would continue until well into 2013 and during all those months, the same agency was monitoring every conversation between me and all employees. That special ops group was also running several other sophisticated eavesdropping and spying programs. They had hacked my surveillance computers, and into my office and personal computers. I have images, of what were literally ghost cables that were spliced into certain aspects of my business operation. In addition, by October 2011, there would constantly be one to two, wireless high tech intelligence gathering balloons over my property 24/7. The balloons were rarely more than several hundred feet up in the air, but were not visible to even photograph, without using specific night vision equipment. We occasionally could detect a weak image on a camera during cloudy days, but like spirits, most people would not see them at all. My neighbor businesses could not see them, even though the balloons were almost directly over their property at times.

Then at 1:45 am that Tuesday morning, I saw things moving around inside my truck that could have only just got into the truck over the last several minutes. J had walked into the lingerie area to get some of her evening tips that she had forgotten to pick up. She was just walking back behind the counter and before I could say anything, she saw what I was looking at on the main monitor. What I was seeing was a short grayish colored extraterrestrial with almost rabbit-like ears, and it was the exact duplicate of a so-called "yoda" character in a past "space wars" movie. I was to encounter nine more of those identical grey creatures over the next four months in my truck and car at different times. Each time I saw them, they appeared as guards who were accompanying several assorted groups of young obviously cloned creatures. Each one of the ten grey look-alikes that I would be in very close proximity to, unlike the one in the movie, was definitely not cute or friendly. They were exactly the same size, maybe 60-80 pounds each and not more than three and one-half to four feet tall. I had confrontations with several of them, as they were trying to restrict where my dog sat in my truck on two occasions. There was one particular event with two of the greys, which always seemed kind of mysterious to me. It happened as I was pulling up to the I-44 entrance toll booth in Miami, Oklahoma. The greys both had appeared in my truck sometime after 4:30 that morning, while it was parked directly under my front door camera at the store. I had stayed overnight alone and had gotten my usual pictures of the entities leaving that morning at 3:45, and I knew that none were in my truck when I went to sleep around 4:30am. Those two had obviously come in through the Portal after I went to sleep, which was quite common. I had to go to Miami to pick up my Rottweiler Sheba from the vet hospital around 10am that morning. As I pulled up to the toll booth as I was leaving Miami, I tersely told the yoda look-alikes that I was going to point them out to the woman in the toll booth. I was looking in my rear view mirror in the truck when they disappeared like lightning, and they never came back to my truck. It was a common occurrence when I was driving through small towns, that two of the adult ETs would leave the vehicle, for fear that I would point them out to someone. However, they would always appear back in the vehicle within several minutes and stare at me like they had outsmarted me. I always wondered what happened to those two greys that morning in Miami at the toll booth.

That Tuesday morning the grey ET was accompanying 8 of the white guinea pig-like creatures, which were going to begin appearing regularly in my vehicles several times a week. Directly behind the rear bumper of my truck was the hybrid in his Grizzly form, and he was standing up very tall and looking back toward the front door of the building. Apparently, the unusual looking gray entity and the smaller white ones had just gotten into the truck, and they were going to be picked up shortly. At that time, we didn't yet know for sure exactly what time the cubicle-like drones were going to arrive. Also, not only did I not know that a Dimensional Portal had opened on the property, but I didn't even yet know what a Portal was. However, I was about to receive a real bounty of very credible information in a couple of days, and it would be a confirmation of what had begun happening on my property. The existence of the Portal and the ramifications of it being on my property, were going to result in certain risks that were going to develop. We would see numerous white and colored lights, which would be streaming in and out of the entire outside area every night in those days. It was exciting each morning to sit down in my office and examine the nightly camera logs, because you never knew what was going to appear on the log. As the morning progressed that Tuesday, J and I had gone outside and looked at the creatures in my truck as well as watching the skies. There were lots of things streaking across the sky near where the Portal was, but I didn't yet know why things were appearing right there. Then just before 3:30am, I took Sheba outside to run around and potty and I was standing near the southwest corner of my building. Right at that time, I saw a group of strange looking lights that were moving toward our property from the west. I saw that the lights were only moving 20 or 30 yards at a time and they would stop, and it appeared that there was three rows of two lights in each row. They all were all moving together, but they were literally just inching along parallel to I-44 coming from the Highway 37 direction. They were not yet onto my property but were very close to our west property line. I would learn by watching them many times over the next five months that the arrangement of lighted cubicles always came from the west along and above I-44, then as they reached the Highway 37 exit they crossed over the interstate. At that point, the yellowish colored cubicles were always in line with the north side highway lights, and their color matched the highway lights color perfectly. That matching color was so critical to their concealment from passing traffic, because the entire group of cubicles would merge into each large highway light as they got to it. It was known that each of the bright yellow I-44 lights was spaced 300 feet apart, along each side of the interstate. It always took a specific number of minutes for the group of cubicles to travel the 100 yards between each light, where they would merge into the highway light and become one. Then within several minutes they would come out of the one light configuration and would then become the individual cubicles form again. That consistent pattern confirmed to me that the entire cubicle orb group was recharging themselves from each highway light. Then after constantly observing nightly I-44 traffic patterns, I determined that the cubicle lights were moving at such a very slow speed, that no one individual driver could detect their movements. I would observe and document the consistent travel patterns of the cubicle-like orbs on an every morning 3:45 AM basis. From that was the exact precise arrival time each morning, the number of minutes required to move between I-44 lights, and a few other characteristics all consistent with recognized military procedure. Before I received outside confirmation, I had already determined from observing the above characteristics, that it was a Level 1 Classified government- military operation. However, the information and advice from others was still extremely crucial to my understanding of things to come. Then one cold rainy night in early January 2012, a highly regarded long time Missouri law enforcement official, would personally deliver a serious message to me. Thankfully, his conversation with me would be overheard by a trusted associate who was beside me.

That morning we pinpointed a pattern that would remain consistent, rain or snow until that specific operation would officially end on December 8, 2011. Only the cloned creatures stopped appearing on that date, but the main two powerful extra terrestrial guards and several other extraterrestrial entities would be in my vehicles 24/7 until a new program began on January 5, 2012. From January 5, 2012 going forward would become the most dangerous and worst year ever in my life, and I would have many close calls. Only God would keep me alive through these extremely perilous times. The operation that began in January was to be solely, an attempt to destroy me in any manner that became available. It would be precisely what I had been warned of in August, that I personally would be targeted because I wouldn't bow to all the threats. That morning as J and I stood outside the front door, it was precisely 3:45 when the six lighted cubicles hovered above her car and my truck, which were both directly in front of the store. We watched as the now quite small entities floated up and into the six cubicles. Just as the very small entities began coming up from my truck, we saw that the six cubicles became instantly twice as bright as they had been. That super whiteness served at least two purposes, first it perfectly hid the creatures within the light, and secondly it allowed the entities to recharge their spiritual bodies. I knew that I had seen the Grizzly earlier, and that meant that he was still close and watching our every move. However, we were never able to see him again that morning and it was only because we didn't interfere with the pickup of the creatures. I could tell he was close, because I could literally feel his powerful spiritual presence around the building. We watched and took pictures of the entities as they entered the cubicles that were not more than 50 feet above my truck. That morning we witnessed a scene that would become an everyday event. It would be something that some other people would have the opportunity to witness over the next five months. We felt that morning that it was going to be ongoing, and we knew without a doubt, that we were witnessing something that was very secretive, and that just watching it could get us killed. The shape of the cubicles had seemed to change as the lights got brighter. They each took on the appearance of oblong shaped orbs, as they slowly moved away in a very uniform attached configuration of the six orbs. They very slowly moved away from my property, as they continued over the B farm to the east for maybe two-hundred yards. Then the entire cubicle configuration of six orbs made a direct turn, back to the north and very slowly went out of sight. It was my belief, that they always left my place on a northerly course and then turned back northwesterly after they got out of my sight. I believed that because it was highly likely that the pickup operation was managed out of the Kellogg Lake area just north of Carthage, Missouri. Also coincidentally, there is a large deep quite sophisticated tunnel system in that area, which is well Marked, Protected, Maintained and Patrolled by U.S. Naval Intelligence Signs. There are previously confirmed reports, of two local individuals running afoul two large extraterrestrials in one of the tunnels several years earlier. There are online records of their 2004 encounter with the ETs in the tunnel system north of Carthage, and from their story it appears to be quite solid. J left around 6am that morning and before that, we had looked at the new creatures that had appeared in my truck after the 3: 45am.pickup. There were eight more of the small white cloned entities along with one guard. That would be the first obvious cloned entity that we had seen as a guard, but certainly would not be the last. This was what appeared to be an 18 years old part human male teenager, who was dressed in a knit type pullover shirt with blue jeans and name - brand sneakers. His head was that of a young elephant with a trunk that was not more than 12-15 inches long. His face and ears were normal human looking, except that his mouth was like an elephants, directly underneath the trunk. He was quite healthy looking otherwise and appeared very athletic, and his arms, hands and legs looked fully human. The one thing that I would always notice about that particular group of elephant head guards was that they seemed to be in training for some tough assignments. There would be numerous more times that I would have those same type individuals accompanying young cloned creatures. However there usually would be several of them together and they were always managed by older looking individuals of different types. I recall at least three different times when Their handlers were dressed in typical Middle-East Arabic attire. My personal belief several years later is that the Arabic dressed males were actually hybrid descendants of fallen angels and Arabic human females. That theory ties directly into my contention of Satan's running the cloning program and managing it with his own kind. I had encountered at least two individuals that had appeared to be direct sons of the Devil himself, little Satans. There would always be different types of clones and guards placed in my autos after midnight and they would often leave the following early morning in the 3:45 AM overhead vehicles. I felt that there were a number of different species of creatures bringing in clones, because the guards and others with them were obviously from totally different worlds it seemed. It became evident later that afternoon, that there were significantly larger numbers of Indian Spirits now in my building and around the outside property. The spirits began a constant vigil of openly harassing the extraterrestrial entities that would be in the vehicles during the day. We watched them daily as that went on, and the entities in the cars were actually very uncomfortable as it happened. The clearly visible interference from the Indian Spirits would cause things that looked like small white drums to float around the vehicles that the ETs were in. I began calling the floating devices tom-toms because that was what they resembled, but I am sure they were powerful spirits that they were using against the ETs. I felt that the white floating objects were each good spirits of some type that were utilized by the Indian Spirits.

It was Tuesday morning and I had been awake again for two days, just as had happened on the past Saturday night. That was a pattern that had begun within days after the May 22 tornado, and my constant loss of sleep would continue that way until early 2013. I had made arrangements for C to work that day, so I was going to be able to get some sleep in my back bedroom before work again that afternoon. I had last been in my bedroom at the store on Saturday evening when I needed to get some change. I had also put a new sheet on the bed at that time, and the sheet was a fitted sheet which fit tightly on the mattress. My bedroom was a constantly locked area, where I kept some types of inventory, change, and many of my personal things. There was no one who had a key to either of the two locks on that door. Tuesday morning around 9, I had gotten a shower and went into my room in back to go to sleep. My room was a very dark area, with dark painted walls which allowed me to get to sleep in the daytime. The room was removed far enough in the back, so that most usual noises didn't wake me. When I unlocked my door that morning and turned on the light, something shiny lying in the middle of the bed caught my attention. There on top of the new sheet was a set of three feathers which were connected to a silver dangle. As I examined it, there was one longer feather with two shorter feathers, and the silver piece separated the two sorter feathers from the one longer one. I knew that no one had been in my room since I was there Saturday evening around 9. I could see that the three feathered configuration was not attached to anything except the silver circular piece. I knew that it had to mean something important within the scope of things that were taking place. I crawled into bed and went to sleep with the three feathers lying next to my pillow. I was really tired and I slept until around 3pm, and I woke up thinking about the feathers. It still didn't make any sense to me at the time, as most things in those days didn't. I got up and went up front with the feathers, but I didn't say anything to C about it. However, at 3:30 precisely, the Indian Dances began as they had the day before at the same time. I showed C what they were doing and had already told her about how it had begun the day before. After she left at 5, a trusted associate of mine came by and I told him about the feathers and showed them to him. I told him I didn't know what they meant, but that

I was going to put them in a top drawer of my desk that stayed locked. With all the strange happenings, I knew that one day I would find out why they had mysteriously appeared. It would be five months to the day in January 2012 when I would know what message the feathers had intended for me. Ironically, that night in January that same associate would be with me when I would understand what the feathers had represented. J wasn't going to be working that night but would be in the next afternoon. I sat in my back office that afternoon and watched the beautiful mystical Indian performance until it ended at 5:30. I knew that the Indian performances were spiritual, and I also believed they had to be directly related to the newly discovered human -animal creature imports. I knew nothing yet of the Portal opening on the west side of my property, nor had I yet learned that the Trail of Tears also was on the west edge also. Never could I have expected those amazing dual blessings, which I was about to receive from two most qualified sources.

Fortunately, that evening business was rather slow, so I began searching the internet for basic possible answers. First, I began looking for information on which Native American Tribe had lived in that area in the past. I had assumed that the spirits performing the Eagle Dances were representative of that local tribe. I discovered that the Delaware Tribe was originally in the northeast part of the United States, and had been pushed into southwest Missouri. They stayed in that Missouri area before being eventually being moved to Bartlesville, Oklahoma in later years. The Turtle Band of the Delaware Tribe had consisted of approximately Eight-Hundred Indians, as they inhabited the area around what was called Centerville. Ironically, the name was changed in 1834 to Sarcoxie, and was actually named after a Shawnee Chief named Sarcoxie. Nevertheless I began searching records of the Turtle Band of the Delaware Tribe, who had lived in the area. I found their tribal website and was able the next day, to begin a dialogue with a member of the Turtle Band Tribal Council.

That Wednesday morning we began discussing the things that were happening with the afternoon Eagle Dance performances. Even though I knew a fair amount about my Native American ancestry, I was going to learn much more from the Delaware Tribe in Bartlesville. What struck me as so interesting was how easily the members of the tribal council accepted my story involving spiritual beings. They would be the first of many Native Americans who I would share my very real spiritual experiences with. From that day forward, I would meet a number of Indians from several different tribes, and I would feel their quick acceptance of me when I engaged them in similar spirit conversations. That discovery would forever make me wonder, why all parents don't teach their children more about the existence of the spirit world, both good and bad. It has never stopped amazing me, how medical professionals could possibly not understand the reality of the spirit world existence. I began speaking with the assistant chief and the other tribal council member in several three-way phone calls. I reported to them every few days, of the strange things that I was witnessing around the grounds of my business. I was first asked how many Indians were always present at the performances, and I told them there was always a minimum of three present. The assured me that that number comprised a legitimate tribal council and it made the event all real. Some of the events that I was relating to them were very strange sounding even to me, and four years later many of those things that I witnessed, are still hard for me to accept. They told me that the council got together and looked up my property location on the map, and they informed me that my property was setting on the edge of the Cherokee Trail of Tears. I then told them of my Cherokee Great Grandmother, and they assured me that things that I had been seeing at night had been spoken of by their ancestors. They also told me that they knew it was all true, because no one else would know of those things. It seemed that one of the tribal council members was quite old, and that he said his grandparents had spoken of only hearing their grandparents discussing witnessing the same events that I was seeing. They were referring to things like us seeing the spiritual entities being put into crystal looking lights, and then exploding and being propelled into the air into Heaven.

I would learn that the spiritual performances that I was witnessing every afternoon, was something that few living have ever witnessed. The Delaware's contention was the spiritual performances, were definitely protests against something that was troubling to God. They explained that the tribal council protests were proof that the extraterrestrials presence was objectionable to God. By the time I got that opinion from them, I had also learned of the Portal that had appeared on my property. I believed that God was definitely against that Portal being used for bringing in those type creatures. As I began telling them more about the human-animal-creature clones that were coming in, there was no doubt why the daily Indian tribal performances were being held there. Many Native Americans have always felt that the so-called aliens were nothing but Satan's own evil creations. Time will prove that his end-time partners are really nothing but Demons, fallen angels, and hybrids. They are what have been mystically described for many years, with innocent sounding descriptions like "cute little blue and green men." I believe that has always been Satan's plan so that when they begin appearing throughout the world, most people will accept them. The media, including certain movie producers, are intentionally assisting in the deception and cover-up, which is being perpetrated against the American People. One of the tribal council members explained to me how important God had always been in the lives of Native Americans. They confided to me that while we may have had different names for Our Father, we still all worshipped the same God. When I started getting visits from powerful Indian Spirits who provided morale and protection, I would understand that they were my ancestors from the Trail of Tears. From the Delaware, I learned that the Delaware and the Cherokee had always had very close relationships. Discussions with my newly discovered cousins, also taught me that I was probably being assisted by powerful spirits from both tribes; the Eastern Band of the Cherokee and the Turtle Band of the Delaware. Additionally, I also guessed that I had help from the Shawnee and Osage Indians, since they too had once lived in the southwest Missouri area. I will always be grateful for the inspiring assistance that I received from the Oklahoma Delaware Tribe in Bartlesville, when my battle was just beginning. I will forever remember how blessed I felt, as I watched all the beautiful Indian Spirits demonstrating their allegiance to God. The most personally gratifying detail of their involvement was that they never appeared night or day unless I was present. That specific detail assured me that one else could actually witness their presence unless I was there. Since I knew that the Indian Spirits were there on God's Behalf, I not only allowed but encouraged others to observe them. I sometimes offered complete strangers the opportunity to witness a phenomenal that few people have ever seen.

That Wednesday morning I realized very early that another overnight shipment of extraterrestrials had appeared in my truck overnight. Since I had gone to sleep soon after closing the night before, I hadn't even attempted to watch the pickup of the young elephant-human guard and his group of identical white clones at 3:45 that morning. However, I could see that they had been picked up and there was a whole new group of entities in their place. I didn't know either of those things until I woke up and looked at the monitor up front. Then when I let Sheba out, we walked over to the driver side of my truck to get a better look at the occupants. That had become a routine for me each and every morning, as I first would look at the monitors to verify that creatures were in my vehicle. Then I would attempt to decide what the new batch looked like before we went up close to them. Each morning it would remind me of Christmas mornings when I was a child, then I was always excited to see the gifts that had mysteriously been left overnight. The drastic difference in this arrangement was that I never ever wanted anything, that was left overnight and I couldn't even return it. Additionally, the ones who were leaving these "gifts", wanted to kill me because I didn't want them using my property as a receiving and shipping point. Worse than that, I believed that these "gifts" were going to ultimately end up intentionally being forwarded throughout the Midwestern States. I also had a strong feeling that similar shipments were simultaneously being delivered to other areas of the United States and throughout the world. The daily influx of entities from the Portal into my vehicles continued, as well as the early morning pickups of the entities from my vehicles. We were getting more than a hundred quality pictures every night alone from the motion activated surveillance cameras. In addition the employees and I were taking hundreds more pictures at night mostly inside and out. When it would all finally wind down, I would have way more than 50,000 images of things that many believe don't exist. One former employee, who was with me for 18 months during those times, would herself take more than 25,000 pictures around and in my buildings.

It was Wednesday, August 10, 2011 and it had become very obvious that I was right in the middle of a top level secret government operation. Every night before midnight, I would see an obviously apparent increase in activity from the bear hybrid. That was happening because the hybrid was attempting to scare me away before the 3:45 AM entity pickups. I had also noticed that whenever the hybrid was close around me in any one of his four forms, I would get pretty severe headaches and congested sinus cavities. I had a close trusted friend who visited me often at night. It wasn't long before I realized that there were hordes of strong paranormal spirits around him, and that they were causing his and my chronic sinus conditions. I got to the point where I could clearly see the mosquito- like spirits that were attacking me. It wouldn't be long, before I would see that a number of other supernatural entities would have the same surrounding them. From that period forward, I would almost constantly keep at least a low grade sinus headache, itchy runny eyes, and other sinus symptoms. Shortly after that, other more painful symptoms began appearing as pain and inflammation in several of my joints, which had previously been injured. Those symptoms would cause me to become quite debilitated at times with severe pains in my knee, neck and shoulders. Those joints had all been injured in different ways over my lifetime, and it actually seemed to me that the ETs knew which joints had been injured. All of my symptoms had for years, and would cause me to have a number of doctor visits. I felt that there was not one physician who believed me, in what I attributed to my symptoms. In 2012 I had an employee began working with me, who became quite closely involved in everything that was still going on with my medical problems. It wouldn't take but a month before she began getting the exact symptoms as I had, except hers would become more serious in a way. I set up a doctor appointment for her for tests, and she was diagnosed with some rare type of Rheumatoid Arthritis that no one in her family had ever had. I knew that her developing these medical problems was not a coincidence by any means, yet no doctor would believe differently. As I explained before, anyone who became truly loyal and knew the truth of what we were experiencing would be medically punished. There would be several other associates of mine, who would suffer varying degrees of similar medical conditions as mine and hers. That was a very definite way that I could measure someone's loyalty and trust in me, because if they were loyal they would be affected by those spirits. I could even measure their degree of loyalty by the type symptoms they incurred. It was always so amazing to me that very few people did get any symptoms, and I only informed the loyal ones of my finding. I theorized from that discovery, that certainly some or maybe all extraterrestrials have the ability to actually measure deep emotional feelings in humans. I saw the solid proof of that theory many times, and I monitored it in a large group of people over a long period of time. Over next more than 18 months of pretty much 24 seven exposure to extraterrestrials, I was able to detect a number of other highly sensitive abilities that they possess. I would have the fortune to meet an individual who was quite knowledgeable in the subject of extraterrestrial life, who would also happen to be a medical doctor. Let me say that our meeting had nothing to do with his medical profession, and I never sought nor received medical advice from him. He would tell me during our very first conversation that "while he wished that he could make them disappear, that hopefully he could help keep me grounded." That was a profound statement from him that would become so relevant, because I was seeing things that most people could not comprehend. However, he would never seem to doubt the validity of my experiences to him. Dr. W would help me greatly in the beginning, by simply explaining to me that ETs would not appear in photographs as they were. However, by the time I was able to actually reach Dr. W, I had been encountering the ETs for almost five months. So I already had discovered numerous times how true his photography information was, but it was a most discouraging issue in my attempt at proving their existence. I knew from the beginning that I was being literally overrun with extraterrestrial entities that many deny are even real. That part of my entire experience with persons denying that I was really dealing with extraterrestrials was the most frustrating feeling. Dr. W correctly explained to me that the ETs would most always appear only as colored lights in the darkness, and as grey blurry fog if at all in the daytime. He knew from the beginning, that I was telling him the truth about my bizarre, unusual encounters, and Dr. W's belief in my unexplainable but true tales was priceless. I have always been quite solid emotionally, but some of the things that I was witnessing could hardly be accepted even as I saw them. Every morning I had to give myself a pep talk about how real it all was, and how focused I must remain in order to prove it to others. My parents use to always tell me that the truth will always come through, and I have told only solid truth from the start. Yet, I had no inkling of how difficult that proof was going to be due to the many years of intense government cover ups of UFO and extraterrestrial existence. I would watch real men get in their vehicles and leave after observing certain strange entities on my property and in my vehicles. Dr. W, as I will call him was also well-connected with other knowledgeable professionals, who also had years of extraterrestrial studies. Dr. W would become someone who I could call on for trusted professional opinions as well as plain advice. In early 2012, he would tell me of a recent conversation that he had, with several of his equally well-versed friends- associates. He had advised me, that he had been updating his associates of my constant month after month interactions with the extraterrestrials. Dr. W had likely also provided the associates with the documentation which I had provided him over several weeks, relating to my daily encounters with a wild assortment of ETs. He told me that based on my information they were pretty much in agreement on two issues. Their first theory was that I may have had had more long-term interaction with extraterrestrials, than anyone else had ever experienced. Secondly, Dr. W and his associates felt that I had shown that all of the ETs were in spirit form, and that may have proven that all extraterrestrials are also in that form. Dr. W would provide me a lot of valuable assistance over the next several years, and he was always there when I called on him. He alone, was able to verify some quite unbelievable things that I was experiencing almost every day. As my spiritual relationship grew stronger with God, I realized that due to Dr. W's unique background, he had definitely been one of God's special gifts to me. I had sent him quite a few pictures of extraterrestrials that I had been taking over a several month period. During that time he and I began having detailed conversations about some of the most unusual things that I was encountering. His past work experience with extraterrestrials and UFOs had been years earlier, while he was part of a special presidential ordered committee. That committee was formed by a newly elected president, who came into office desiring to know as much as possible about our government's relationship with extraterrestrials. I had already had the fortune to discuss my ongoing ET encounters with a couple of other quite knowledgeable individuals. Ironically, one of those individuals was well versed in situations such as I was involved in. He would be able to advise me of the pitfalls relating to my attempts to uncover things. That same individual also well understood the cover up ramifications. When I finally reached Dr. W on December 20, 2011, I knew by the end of our nearly two hour phone conversation, that he was also going to be a great asset to me. He never disappointed me with his always forthright opinion on what I was experiencing. I called him several times from January until middle February when I realized that I was being physically attacked by small blue, green and grey ETs. Then there were several different nights that I was aware of, when I was very nearly abducted out of my vehicles as I drove home with my two brave loyal dogs. My two large dogs were constant targets of the more spiritually powerful extraterrestrials, who I believed felt more threatened by the dogs than by me. There was a night in late December 2011, when my son from Tulsa had come up to my Missouri office. It was after 1am when we started to the farm in Oklahoma, and he had left his car at my office and was riding in my truck. I have two separate gates going through the farm road into my house. That night my two horses were in a pasture close to the house, so we had to open the second gate. As I was getting out of the truck opening the gate, I heard noise like a large tarp flapping in the wind. In those days, I always kept my main digital camera lying on the dash in the vehicle that I was in. I was accustomed to having to take pictures quickly, so as usual I grabbed my camera. Something very large was coming up out of the bed of my truck, which was like nothing that I had ever seen. I had seen enough dinosaur pictures in school to know, that I was witnessing two Pterodactyls that were coming up out of my truck. They went up to maybe 30-40-feet feet high and were slowly flying across my large front yard. Each of them had probably a 12 to 16 feet wingspread ,and their head and vicious looking teeth, left no doubt as to what I was witnessing. I took several pictures as they were first leaving and the images were only one of two groups of colored lights in each picture. My son wanted to know what it was, and I told him that it was two Pterodactyls that came out of my truck. Of course, my son couldn't see them, and my wife had constantly told my children that I was imagining things that didn't exist. I stood beside my truck and watched both dinosaurs as they began gliding the last several hundred yards into the big timber behind my home. Two days later in a phone conversation with Dr. W, I related that experience to him. He told me that there had been evidence of Pterodactyls, being in one of the more evil worlds that his former committee had known of. The most obvious reason that my property was being used was the Portal's existence on it. One obvious reason it was chosen, was that the entire building and three acres property was well below the field of view of most drivers passing on the interstate. However soon after the individual advised me of the Portal and who was utilizing it, I devised a maneuver that would prevent the entities from being picked up from out of my automobiles. I wouldn't begin using that plan until the middle of September, and it would drive the programmed government handlers crazy trying to get around my plan, but they couldn't stop me from successfully using it every time I wanted. By October 5 they would have a plan in place, which would temporarily prevent me from exposing the government's extraterrestrial cloning program to a major news source. They had arranged to have the local sheriff arrest me on a totally bogus charge, and then hold me in jail until the entities could be removed from my vehicles. They would arrest me just before the international tabloid crew would fly into Springfield the next day. They were going to hold me in a jail cell without a bond on a "48 hour mandatory mental health hold." Then on Friday October 7 at 4:50 pm after holding me for 47 hours and 50 minutes, a mental health physician showed up at the jail to examine me. Directly after a 5 minute meeting with me, in my presence the Joplin mental health doctor tersely wrote her diagnosis. On a full legal pad page that she tore from the binder, the Female Psychiatrist hurriedly scratched in large bold print the following statement; THERE IS NO EVIDENCE OF MENTAL ILLNESS! As the jail official watched, the doctor most cordially apologized to me for my inconvenience. She turned and threw the statement on the desk and abruptly walked out with a most disgusted look on her face. There was no doubt in my mind that she had seen a similar scenario before. I would still spend another 18 hours in the jail before I would get out. Several days later in a court appearance, I would tell the district judge a little bit about my arrest. Without me even having an attorney present, that honest judge would instruct me to get a motion to dismiss him and he would dismiss that bogus case against me. I did and the judge kept his word. Glory To God! Th government had allowed the seven cloned creatures to be removed from my two vehicles in my parking lot. That would prevent the international news organization from physically observing human-animal and human-swordfish clones that were in both of my vehicles that day on October 5. The existence of the entities in my vehicles had already been verified, and the news crew had scheduled an afternoon flight the next day. Their New Jersey office was to notify me that afternoon of their flight schedule into Springfield, but I was taken away from my business before I got the flight information. The phones in my store had stopped working that morning right after 10am, and I was taken out of my business within two hours after that. I would not get back into my business until late Saturday afternoon. I knew that I had just experienced the second attempt by the government ET babysitters to get a mental illness diagnosis. I didn't realize how many more times they would attempt the same routine again, but it would be in different settings. Satan and his frog-like demons had stolen 15 Million Dollars from me that October 5, 2011, that would not be all he had stolen out of my life. Satan is the father of all lies, Satan is the destroyer, Satan is a well-known thief. Jesus warned us well of who the devil is.

God would clearly tell me on August 10, what the Beasts position was in the everyday operation. I would learn that night, that he was the onsite enforcer and coordinator who was responsible for the protection of the cloned entities. His only duty was to safeguard the operation throughout each twenty-four hour period. Each period began with the arrival via the Portal, of a new shipment of human-nonhuman clones, and ended once the entities were safely transferred to the orb-like cubicles overhead. At that same time God would tell me, that there were two supernatural powerful frog-looking extraterrestrials Demons, who were bosses over the Beast. The two of them would always be together in my vehicles, and they first appeared to me on that night of August 10. He would tell me that those two were in charge of running the clone import operation, but that their boss was a more supernatural powerful individual, who had begun the plan thousands of years ago. It would be a little while before I would be able to put it all together, but on September 25 I would meet that mastermind behind the human-animal cloning program. He was also in charge of the extraterrestrials in other worlds, that he was trying to flood the earth with. He would be the Cherubim who had always wanted to take the place where Christ would be seated, at the Right Hand of the Father. Because of that greed, he had been kicked out of Heaven along with one-third of the angels who chose to follow him at the end of the First Earth Age. In the beginning of the Second Earth Age which we are in now, in the Garden of Eden Satan had beguiled Eve in an attempt to pollute the purity of the seed line from which Christ would come. At that time, God had sentenced Satan to death, and he and his fallen angels were bound and held by powerful angels of God. However, Satan's powerful spirit would still abound throughout the world and he would continue to create evil. Satan would still devise many more attempts, over the next several thousand years to take the place of Christ. Apolyon, another name for Satan, would also be directly responsible for causing the death of Jesus Christ on a cross. His intent now to flood the earth, with his demons, hybrids, and fallen angels will be his final futile attempt to avoid the fiery death that God promised him. His death in the consuming fire of our God will surely happen after the end of this Second Earth Age. Satan was the individual who was in spirit form, in my car on August 7 that ended up in my home in Oklahoma. He would also be the one who is now in command of an evil, arrogant, highly secretive, business arrangement with our government. One of the most secretive agencies within our government, literally crawled in bed with Satan more than 60 years ago, and is now helping Lucifer carry out his end time attempt to thwart the Will of God. We are a country that was built upon our Faith in God, and we have received immeasurable blessings from Him for more than two-hundred years. We are now spending billions of dollars annually on nurturing, disguising and denying our relationship with Satan's Demons. For this reason, we are complicit in Satan's final attempt of the overthrow of God's Kingdom. Therefore, it should be no surprise, that the disclosure of the human-creature cloning program would be an abomination to Christians around the world. However, God assures us that Satan's final plan will fail just as his others have, but this time Satan will be destroyed in the consuming fire. God also clearly shows us, that all of those who have conspired with and followed him will suffer that same fate.

Then on October 10, God told me that I had to destroy the Beast in God's Words; "I had to destroy him in order to gain me some credibility in this world." He promised that "He would let me know when it was time and that He would help me." Then just as He had promised the time came at 12 Noon on December 7, 2011, Pearl Harbor Day, when I pulled over and stopped on the highest hill in Anderson, Missouri. An older man was burning leaves in his yard, and he watched it all from fifty yards away as Sheba and I fought the supernatural Beast. Then as God had promised me two months earlier, I did as He told me and beside me in the middle of the road, the Hybrid was instantly consumed by fire. For four months nearly 24/7, I and my Sheba had fought with that seven and one-half foot beast and sometimes 250-pound Timber Wolf. We had fought them in the store building and in the vehicles while I was driving, but the worst times were around my farm night and day. Over the next fourteen months, God would allow me to witness up close a number of times that same awesome consuming fire. I not only would be allowed to see it, but my same compassionate Heavenly Father would also allow me to be a partner in the destruction of a number of other supernatural enemies. The man who was burning leaves had watched from the time that I pulled my truck off the road. He came over and asked me if I was okay, I remember only smiling and assuring him that I was okay. I knew that he would not believe what he had just witnessed, because I found it hard to believe too. I instantly realized that it had been exactly four months from the date when had I first encountered the Hybrid. Even more meaningful it was two months after the date in October, when God had told me that I had to kill the Hybrid in order to gain credibility in that world. I was about ten miles from my place in Oklahoma and it was a little past noon on December 7, and I intended to be back to the store by 6pm. That night I was going to have an awesome encounter, which would truly be another of my real Star Wars type experiences. There were going to be many more of those same type of unbelievable incidents, which would seem taken right out of the scenes of those familiar science fiction movies. Many of those events would seem so precisely similar to scenarios appearing in certain space wars type movie scenes, that it solidly convinced me of only one conclusion. It would just about guarantee, that the creators and producers of those specific films had been provided much extensive insider information. They would have had to have been provided with actual photographs and many other unique details, concerning a number of known types of extraterrestrial life. My contention was based upon my numerous up-close encounters with exact unique looking and acting and sounding creatures, which have appeared in certain movies over the last forty years. Even the same mannerisms including specific sounds and habits, were evident in the entities I was around. I believe that it proves without a doubt, that the citizens of this country are being denied the truth, about extraterrestrial programs that an agency of our government has been deeply involved in. The real irony is that at the same time, a few of the best-connected citizens are allowed to profit from knowing that truth that we are all denied. Even worse, many patriotic American citizens have suffered untimely destruction of their lives over the last 60 years for only trying to expose that same truth. I had once early on said to God;" God this is like being in Star Wars" and God clearly replied" THIS IS the REAL STAR WARS." God had explained to me, the relevance of that Beast authority under Satan. Satan called the shots, but the Beast was the overseer of the alien cloning operation. However the most powerful and evil are the Three Evil Spirits in Revelations called the Unclean Spirit-like Frogs mentioned in Revelations 16: 13—14. These are the powerful frog-like demons who stole the Nordish ETS from my truck on October 5, 2011, and are the most powerful frog-like demons that come out of the mouths of the Dragon, The False Prophet, and the Beast. These unclean spirits do miracles to deceive the kings of the earth to gather for a final battle against God Almighty. These demons set up the ultimate confrontation between the one who claims to be all mighty and the God who is the All Mighty. I had watched them change into skeletons right before my eyes and attacked my Rottweiler, early morning at 3:45 on December 8, 2011, the morning after the Beast was killed. Sheba was injured badly that morning from the poison vials that they carried. Those Three Frog-like Demons have another role in the end of Revelations, that is one of the stranger images in the entire book.

www.ingramcontent.com/pod-product-compliance
Lightning Source LLC
Chambersburg PA
CBHW060417310726
48976CB00003B/1085